Sigmund

by

Valerie Baxter

Strategic Book Publishing and Rights Co.

Copyright © 2016 Valerie Baxter. All rights reserved.

No part of this book may be reproduced or transmitted in any form or by any means, graphic, electronic, or mechanical, including photocopying, recording, taping, or by any information storage retrieval system, without the permission, in writing, of the publisher. For more information, send an email to support@sbpra.net, Attention: Subsidiary Rights.

Strategic Book Publishing and Rights Co., LLC
USA | Singapore
www.sbpra.com

For information about special discounts for bulk purchases, please contact Strategic Book Publishing and Rights Co., LLC. Special Sales, at bookorder@sbpra.net.

ISBN: 978-1-68181-391-2

This book is dedicated to the men and women who, without any thought for their own safety, are giving their lives and service to their country, and also to those who have given their lives in the past and to the ones who will do so in the future.

Chapter 1

It was May 1941 at 2:00 a.m., and my heart was thudding nearly as loudly as the drone of the small aircraft's engine as we crossed over the last bit of the English Channel into French airspace. I was both terrified and exhilarated as the time for the plane's quick landing and quick departure approached, leaving me to run for cover and wait for my contact to give me the previously arranged signal.

I was well trained in wireless operations and espionage, and I was fluent in German and in French, my second language, but I was still full of trepidation about my ability to be of help to the resistance, help they desperately needed.

My name is Nicole Du Bois and I am twenty-five years old. My father, a Frenchman, had spoken to me in French since my birth, which makes me perfect in oral and written French. My parents do not know of this operation—only that I joined the RAF. Arrangements had been made for my parents to receive occasional letters from me, posted mainly in the United Kingdom.

We owned a small house in Blois where I spent a lot of my childhood. I intended to live there and behave outwardly as an ordinary local citizen whilst sending radio messages that give positions and other information about the Nazis. I would assist in carrying out acts of sabotage against them, aid in the escape of prisoners of war, and notify the resistance of any traitor in their midst, something I hoped I would never have to do.

"Two minutes to touch down," came the voice of the pilot as we saw small, flickering lights to guide the pilot in. "Chuck your case out first, jump, and then retrieve your case and run like hell away from the aircraft. Make sure you run to the left and aim for the cover of the trees. Good luck."

As soon as the wheels touched down the other passenger opened the door, threw out his haversack, and jumped out. I followed suit, first my case and then myself. As I had been taught, I rolled in order to break my fall when I hit the ground. In fact, I was still pretty winded. I retrieved my case and ran as fast as I could away from the plane, which was already taking off, and kept to the left towards the treeline as instructed. I had no idea where my travelling companion went. We were given strict instructions not to converse with each other. All I knew was that he didn't run to the left!

I fell headlong into the undergrowth of a small copse and hid as best I could to wait for the signal, the snapping of brittle twigs at three-second intervals, six times. All I could hear at first was my heavy breathing from the effort of running hard while carrying my heavy case. Gradually my breathing became normal and I settled down, staying alert for strange sounds and, of course, my contact's signal. This would not come soon as it was vital that my contact made sure there was no immediate danger. It seemed absolutely ages before I heard the six loud snap of twigs at three-second intervals, which I answered by snapping a reasonably sized twig once. Of course, my contact knew exactly where I was.

A dark shape approached my position and whispered, "Nicole."

I stood up and the man took my case and beckoned for me to follow him. We walked through the woods in complete silence until we came to a derelict barn and entered. There were three more men there. My contact, whose name was Claude, introduced them. The other three were Pierre, a young, skinny lad; Gerrard, a man in his late fifties; and Maurice, a man probably in his thirties with a significant limp who was handsome and well built.

Claude came close and said, "I am afraid you must send a radio message right away to say that the package has been picked up and two packages safely delivered. The most vital message is to report that the Nazis have information about the movement of one of the battalions of English and French troops, and they must move immediately."

After I sent the messages, Claude drew me aside and whispered, "It is possible that we have a traitor amongst us—not necessarily in our cell but somewhere close by, but we must assume it is someone close to us."

Claude and I then left, and the other three dispersed to their respective posts. My next move would be to get my radio and me to Blois where I would stay at my family home. I would meet up again with the rest once I had settled in and got the lay of the land. My cover story was that I had been living in Paris with my husband, who had left me and was now living somewhere in the Alps. His name was Gilbert le Saux. The details of my story could be verified if someone checked.

Blois, a fair sized country town, was about ten kilometres from the drop zone, and I was to wait until midmorning before going there. The risk, of course, was that I had my radio in my case, and if I was stopped I had no legitimate excuse for carrying one.

In actual fact, all went well.

Chapter 2

I settled in quite easily. My neighbour seemed a little suspicious but soon came round when I spoke of my parents whom she had known since I was a child. Her name was Blanche and she had lived in Blois all her life. Blanche had been widowed for ten years and her only son had joined up and was fighting with the allies.

When she enquired about my marital status, I explained my circumstances. I had come here because I could no longer live in Paris in the house my husband and I shared after the Nazis had requisitioned it.

I started uncovering the small amount of furniture that was there and dusting off the cobwebs. I lit a fire and dragged the mattress down. I propped it up in front of the fire to air out the dampness that had come from being in an empty house for so long.

I went into the backyard—the only outside space that belonged to the house. There was no actual boundary fence, just a mishmash of garden pots and urns containing dead plants and shrubs. At the edge of our land, a steep bank led to a railway line, one that was barely used. Hidden in the yard behind old fruit boxes, flowerpots, and broken garden furniture was a trapdoor leading to a small cellar filled with all kinds of detritus. There was no access into the house as the previous owners had bricked up the entrance.

There was also an outside privy, the hole in the ground type, that my father had boxed in and made into a kind of unit from one side of what was really no more than a shed to the other. He had incorporated a seat with a lid directly over the hole. It was pungent to say the least, but I decided that this would be an ideal place to hide my radio, I would keep it as stinky as possible. It entered my mind that this should have been the first thing I did in case someone checked up on me. It should have been my priority. I must be more careful. Making sure Blanche was not about; I got the radio and put it under the toilet seat as faraway from the hole as possible so there was no chance of it falling in.

I went inside and washed. Then I made myself some bread and cheese and drank a glass of fresh milk, the only provisions available locally, apart from the eggs that I had purchased from the small grocer that was virtually depleted of provisions.

After my repast, I dragged the mattress up the stairs, a much harder feat than dragging it down, and put on the sheets I had brought with me and the moth-eaten and slightly gnawed blankets that I had also aired. I lit a small fire in the bedroom and opened the window a tad, to warm the room without causing too much condensation.

I had only just finished when there was a loud thumping on the door. I ran downstairs and opened the door to find two storm troopers standing there. They pushed past me without saying a word and started searching the house with no finesse whatsoever. They completely ignored me and carried on a conversation between themselves obviously having no idea that I could understand them.

"Bit of all right this one, isn't she?" said one of them throwing off the chair cushions.

"Well, I would certainly give her one," said the other laughingly.

They proceeded into the yard and started kicking things over and out of their way. One of them put his head inside the privy and immediately recoiled.

"Bloody hell, it absolutely stinks in there. Not a hygienic lot the French, are they?" said the other nearly gagging.

They went back inside and asked, in French if they could see my papers. They checked them thoroughly, handed them back, and left. I tidied up as much as possible, but I was so tired that I cleaned my teeth and went to bed, snuggling in the warm sheets. The little fire had certainly made a vast difference and I fell asleep immediately.

The following morning I woke early to a lovely morning with a blazing sun. There was a little chill in the air, but, of course, it was still only May. After my wash, I got dressed and went into the yard. Blanche was in her yard. I told her of my visit from the Germans, and she told me that the Germans had their local headquarters at the Chateau. It was occupied by the Gestapo, the secret political police created by Goering when the Nazis came to power in 1933. (Simultaneously Heinrich Himmler, head of the SS, the Nazi paramilitary corps, was given command over Goering's Gestapo in April 1934. In June 1937 Himmler also took control of all Germany's police forces.) Apparently there were quite few "big-wigs" billeted there, but as to who they were Blanche had no idea, but they were certainly swanning it in this beautiful building.

"Do they employ locals, Blanche?" I enquired.

"Yes, but it is not looked on favourably by the majority of the local townspeople. You would not want to work there, Nicole, would you? You would be working for our enemy," Blanche said incredulously.

"I have to earn some money, Blanche. I am virtually broke and have nothing to live on."

"Of course, this is entirely up to you, but I for one am against it." Blanche turned on her heels and went inside. I think I made my first enemy!

I had made up my mind as soon as I heard that the Gestapo was installed in the Chateau. What an opportunity to pick up useful information, information that could be vital to the resistance and the allies.

Chapter 3

On 11 May 1941, dressed in my most flattering outfit, I walked to the beautiful Chateau. Strong memories of my youth came flooding back as I entered the huge, ornamental iron gates that were now left open for the sinister looking large black Citroen cars, favoured by the Gestapo, to roar in and out. As a child I used to walk round the gardens, a luxury permitted by the owners at that time to all villagers, and imagine that my family lived there.

A Nazi soldier stopped me at the entrance and, in an aggressive tone, asked what I was doing there and what I wanted. After I explained the reason to him in German, he picked up a phone and spoke to someone inside the house. After he put the phone down, he told me to wait by the beautiful oak doors at the top of the steps, and someone would come and speak to me. He checked my papers, of course.

After a considerable amount of time, a female officer, of some rank or other, opened the door and told me to enter. My papers were again checked, and the officer asked me about my qualifications and what I was doing in the area. After explaining it to her in perfect German, she told me to take a seat and strode off, her large calves bulging and her large buttocks seeming to hold a boxing match beneath her skirt. I nearly laughed out loud but managed to control myself.

I must have been sitting there for at least an hour before anyone came back. This time it was a fat bellied, rather scruffy individual who introduced himself as Major Schultz. I immediately labelled him as lecherous because he nearly drooled as he stared at my breasts, which I must admit were a little on show. He led me into an office where another obviously high-ranking officer sat behind a beautifully ornate French desk. He introduced himself as SS-Obersturmbannführer (Lieutenant Colonel in English) Sigmund Lubisch. I must say he was one of the handsomest men I had ever seen.

"What is your name?"

"Nicole du Bois," I answered clearly and confidently.

"Well, Nicole, what can I do for you?"

"I was wondering, Sir, if there are any clerical jobs available. I have good knowledge of accounting and can do most clerical jobs, including typing. I am fluent in German and, of course, my native French. I can speak a little English, but I am afraid it is rather poor. My husband, Gilbert du Saux, left me in Paris with no money and nowhere to live, so I have come back to live in my old family home. I believe he now lives in the Alps with his new lover, but I have no idea where. I need to get employment."

Lubisch, I can't keep giving him his impressive title, sat quietly, not taking his beautiful, deep-blue eyes off my face whilst I gave my historical report. He eventually turned to Schultz.

"We need someone to order provisions and do general filing, housekeeping, accounting, and other things, don't we?"

"I believe we do, Sir."

"Well, Nicole, we are not fools. We will have to carry out checks on your background. I would like you to leave your papers with me for the time being."

"What will happen if I get stopped? I won't have proof of identity to show," I said, putting a worried look on my face.

"If you obey the rules and are not out after curfew, you have nothing to worry about," Lubisch said coldly. "Go now and someone will get in touch with you in due course." Lubisch rose from his seat and clicked his heels.

I made my way back, stopping at the little provision store to see what was available. I was able to buy herbs, a few vegetables, a little homemade butter and cheese, fresh milk, flour, yeast, eggs, salt, and a chicken. I was lucky enough to get a little coffee too. I felt quite pleased with myself when I arrived home and unpacked my goodies. There were enough supplies for me to make several meals, and I was particularly good at making bread.

I finished off the bread and cheese that was left from the previous evening and drank some beautiful fresh milk. I wondered whether I would still be able to get provisions locally once the villagers found out I was working at the Chateau if, indeed, I got a job there. I A letter would be sent to my parents telling them I was fine but would not be in touch for some time, because I was being transferred abroad to help with translating documents vital to the war effort.

I carried on with tidying up the mess left by the two soldiers after their ransacking search of my house and then went into the yard, armed with disinfectant, a bucket of water, a brush, and some straw. This was to make Blanche think I was about to clean the privy when, in fact, I was going to make access to the radio easier. I removed some panels, farther away from the hole, approximately where I thought the radio was, and I was nearly spot-on.

I sang as I worked although the stench kept catching in my throat and I could not help but retch. I made a loose trapdoor that could be lifted out in an emergency, and then covered it up with anything smelly and messy that I could get my hands on, heaving continually, so that it looked completely untouched and matched the majority of my father's handiwork in the privy. I even managed to get a clump of cobwebs to help with the camouflage. I washed and cleaned the seat and stuck a handful of straw down the hole. Of course, all of this would be destroyed if I had to access the radio. I was actually pleased with the results and my day's work.

After having something to eat and a cup of coffee, which I had been looking forward to all day and that actually tasted like it had been recycled, I started to read a book. Unfortunately, I could not keep awake long enough to finish the first chapter, so I went to bed.

I was in a deep sleep only to be awakened by a hand clasped firmly over my mouth and Claude's voice saying we had to send a radio message as soon as possible. I was out of bed and dressed in dark clothing in record time. I collected the radio, making sure there were no signs of life in Blanche's house. Claude and I slipped down the railway bank, after having crawled along the top of the bank away from the vicinity of my house, and found Gerrard and Pierre already there waiting for us.

Pierre led the way in complete silence across the track and into the woods, often putting his hand up for us to stop and listen. After about a half a mile we stopped and waited silently for some time. Finally, Claude told me to send the message. The message to our contact said that a resistance cell in the Tours area had been infiltrated, and they were not to go ahead with the already arranged drop.

This referred to an escaped prisoner, an RAF lad, who would have to remain hidden until we could find another place for him to be picked up. Passing him on to the Tours cell would be dangerous and a risk to his life if, indeed, they had a traitor in their midst; so Claude and his men would hide the lad. Claude also asked me to radio that the fishing was good at La Rochelle, a big U-Boat port. This meant that there was a suspected traitor amongst one or more of the local cells.

Once the message had been sent, I told Claude that I had applied for a job at the Chateau and thought this would be beneficial as I might glean some useful information. Claude made no comment but squeezed my hand, a gesture that I took to be a seal of his approval. We made our way back via a different route, and as I clambered up the bank, Claude pushed the radio behind me, smoothing out any sign of movement on the bank.

Once I had stowed away the radio I went into the kitchen, had a thorough "strip wash," put away my dirty clothes, and got into bed. If the radio message was intercepted and there was a raid, it would appear as if I had not left my bed. In fact, nothing happened and I got a few hours' sleep and woke to another beautiful spring morning. As I was getting up, there was a banging on the door. I opened it to find the same two soldiers that had ransacked my house two days before standing there.

They handed me a letter that I took inside, leaving the door open and the soldiers standing there obviously waiting for a reply. It was from Lubisch inviting me to start a job at the Chateau as a general clerk. It stated that many staff members in the clerical department were local residents. He requested that I start that afternoon because there was a French document to translate. This was obviously a test.

I wrote a note in German, thanking Lubisch for the job and saying that I would be there at 2:00 p.m. I added my sincere thanks for the opportunity, but I felt like throwing up. I handed the letter to the soldiers and they left.

Chapter 4

At 1:30 p.m. on Monday, 12 May, I dressed to the nines and left my little house. My fair hair gleamed and smelled of lemon. Rinsing your hair in fresh lemon juice to enhance the blondeness and shine was a trick taught to me by grandmother. My makeup was discreet but immaculately applied. All in all, I was pretty pleased with myself.

I arrived at the Chateau gates, where the same soldier stood sentry. He was obviously expecting me as he did not enquire after my papers or ask why I was there. I saw appreciation of my appearance in his eyes when he told me to go to the front door. As I approached the door, it opened and the same female officer told me to follow her. I kept my eyes on my surroundings. I dared not look at her backside in case I could not control myself this time.

We went to a large office where several girls and women were apparently busy folding leaflets. The officer, whom I now knew as Schmitz, showed me to a large desk where there were several files printed with the logo of the local Marie (town hall). I was instructed to translate the contents of each file into German. I nodded, sat down, and started with the first file. It was minutes of meetings from before the war and had no significant content. It was mainly planning applications, border disputes, and the upkeep for roads, woods, and rivers. There were applications for fishing permits and all things of that ilk. It took me the rest of the afternoon to translate the contents of the first file, which was extremely boring.

At 5:00 p.m. we were supplied with a cup of coffee, real coffee, and it was delicious. As I was standing at the table with several of the women, Major Schultz appeared. He came straight up to me, put his hand up my skirt, and grabbed my crotch. I swung round automatically and punched him straight in the face. Of course, he reciprocated with a much harder blow. My silk shirt was covered in blood from my profusely bleeding nose. Luckily my nose was not broken, but I would have two black eyes.

"You French whore," Schultz spat. "You will be sorry, don't you worry."

"Sorry for what?" Lubisch asked as he entered the room, his eyes taking in my sorry state. "What the hell has happened here, Schultz?"

"Subordination, Sir, she had to be taught a lesson."

"Excuse me, I was not subordinate. You sexually assaulted me without provocation, and I will not be touched in such a way by you or anybody," I said furiously, without giving thought to the consequences of talking to a German officer in such a manner.

Lubisch looked at me without obvious emotion and indicated that Schultz follow him into his office. The rest of the women helped me clean myself up, luckily my nose had stopped bleeding, and one of the women produced a cotton blouse that I gratefully changed into. I washed my lovely silk blouse in cold water and hoped that all the blood would come out, although I did not hold out much hope.

About half an hour later, Schmitz came and asked me to go see Lubisch. This I obviously did and knocked on his office door. There was quite a delay before he told me to come in. I stood in front of his desk whilst he looked me up and down. He then told me to take a seat which I did as I felt a little weak.

"Major Schmitz has given me an account of what happened, but there is no way I can condone your striking a German officer," Lubisch said sternly.

"I am not going to be groped by Major Schultz or anybody **else**. I was defending myself and would do so again if the situation arose. I may be classed as the enemy, but I am a human being, a well bred and well educated one at that."

"Well, if you have finished your work for the day, I think you should go home and get cleaned up. We will see you again tomorrow when you can make a fresh start."

Lubisch put his head down and started getting on with whatever was on his desk. Obviously, I was being dismissed. I was absolutely furious. Although I was the aggrieved party, I was not going to receive any apology from that fat slob Schultz.

When I got home that evening, Blanche, who was watering the plants in front of her house, snubbed me. I felt quite weepy but only because I was still livid about the events of that afternoon. I made myself a meal and had a wash and decided to put my nightdress and dressing gown on. I lit the fire although it was not that cold, but I needed some comfort. I started reading my book but must have dropped off, because the next thing I felt was Claude shaking me.

"Nicole, Nicole, we have to send an urgent message. It will have to be sent from here; we have no time to spare!"

I got the radio from the privy and sent the message Claude dictated. It was a coded message, a code that I did not know, which meant it was of the utmost secrecy, and I knew better than to ask questions. Claude said there would most likely be repercussions because the radio message would be traced to the local area. When Claude left, I hid the radio in the privy, making as sure as I could that there was no sign that anything untoward had occurred on my premises. I had to wash thoroughly again so there was no residual smell from the radio. I got into bed and fell asleep; however, not for long.

I knew immediately what was happening when I heard the engines of trucks, motorbikes, cars and the unmistakable sound of hobnail boots. People were shouting and screaming as men, women, and children were being dragged from their homes. My front door burst open and two German soldiers dragged me from my bed and out into the road, where they pushed me in the middle of the ever-increasing group of people. I had a few strange looks as my face was now showing a large bruise around my nose where Schultz had hit me. Blanche was there and asked, rather slyly, if I knew what was going on. I told her that I had no idea. The soldiers were going into every house searching, and from the sound of things, were not being very careful about it.

It was quite a chilly morning, and we all stood huddled together in our nightwear trying to get warm. My nightdress left little to the imagination, as did the clothing of a few others, and the troops made no secret that they were enjoying the sight of our bodies through the flimsy material. Blanche turned to me.

"You started work at the Chateau, so I suppose you knew this was going to happen." This was spoken with malice, and several others heard what she had to say. "How did you receive that bruise? Were they trying to get information from you?"

"No, they were not trying to get information from me and as I have already told you, Blanche, I had absolutely no prior knowledge about this search and what it is for. Don't try to make more trouble for us by trying to turn us against one another. I told you I have no money and had to get a job. It so happens that I speak German and that is why I went to the Chateau to ask for employment. Does that satisfy your curiosity?"

Blanche seemed to sneer as she turned away, raising her eyebrows to the villagers that were near her.

"Nicole is not the only one of us working there, Blanche," said another villager. Blanche completely ignored this.

My house was the next to be subjected to the search. I prayed that I had hidden the radio well enough so they would not find it and that the privy still stank like hell. It seemed forever before the soldiers emerged.

"Whose house is this?" asked one of the soldiers. My heart was fluttering ten to the dozen, but I managed to say calmly that it was mine.

"You should clean your privy, it is disgusting."

I was so relieved and took no notice of the soldiers gawking at my body. All that mattered was that they had not found the radio. At this juncture, Lubisch turned up and explained to the crowd that a radio message had been sent from this vicinity during the night and that two villagers would be arrested and held until the culprit was found. He turned towards me and his eyes took in every part of my body with obvious pleasure. Two elderly men were taken into custody and driven to the Chateau for imprisonment.

"The rest of you go home and think sensibly. If the culprit is not found or given up within two weeks, both prisoners will be executed. I never break my word." Lubisch's final sentence was said with such menace that we all knew it was likely that these two poor souls would be executed as I was the only one to be able to admit guilt..

I went into my house, made a hot drink, washed, dressed, and then made my way to the Chateau. By now, it was gone 10:00 a.m. I went straight to my desk and started the translation of another boring file. Lunch was supplied, a real luxury, as none of us had much in the way of food at our homes. Today was soup, bread, and a chunk of cheese followed by a cup of proper coffee.

When I got back to my desk, Major Schultz came over to me. My skin started to crawl, but he was only there to tell me to go to Lubisch's office right away. He still wore that lecherous look, which left me with no doubt that he would chance his luck again. I went to Lubisch's office, knocked, and was told to enter.

"Hello, Nicole. Are you feeling better? You certainly have a nasty bruise on your face. Anyway, less of the chitchat, I have a proposition to offer you. It is something that you will have to think very seriously about. I would like you to move into the Chateau and help us to find out about anybody on the outside who is working against us, since most people would not suspect you."

Sigmund

This could not be better, I thought. *I will be able to help the resistance much more with information that I hope to glean by working and living at the Chateau.*

"Thank you. Obviously, I will have to consider this very carefully. I am already under suspicion by some of the villagers, but I promise I will think most seriously about it. Can I have a few days?"

"Of course, Nicole. Perhaps you can let me know at the end of the week." His tone of voice told me the conversation was over.

I managed to work for the rest of the day whilst being filled with such excitement. I could not wait to tell Claude, but I wondered where I was going to hide my radio. As soon as I got home I used a pre-arranged signal to let one of the cells know that I needed to see Claude as a matter of urgency. I noticed Pierre go by on his bike and knew that Claude would be visiting me tonight. Claude arrived at about 1:00 a.m. I told him of the proposition given me by Lubisch and pointed out the advantages and, of course, the disadvantages, mainly how I would be able to make contact whilst living at the Chateau, especially if I was moved. Claude and I discussed the pros and cons and decided that it would be a good opportunity.

I already had a little information to pass on. I told Claude that there was quite a lot of coming and going of naval officers from the U-boat base at La Rochelle. Claude said he would pass this on as it could well be of significance and said he was very pleased that I was a member of his cell. He warned me that it was a dangerous game I was playing and to be on my guard at all times, even with people I knew. I told him I would be moving into the Chateau at the end of the week and would find a hiding place for the radio.

Claude said good night and squeezed me tight. "Take care," he said"

Chapter 5

When my mind was made up, I asked to see Lubisch.

"I am so pleased that you have made the decision to work for me, Nicole. I am sure you will prove invaluable."

"I do hope so," I said as genuinely as I could and thought, *little do you know*!

I moved into the Chateau 15 May. I was given a small, pleasant room at the top of a small flight of stairs and was told that I must keep my door at the top of the staircase open at all times. I unpacked my belongings and put them away in a compactum. I had left my radio where it was in the privy for the time being but would have to move it as soon as I could.

That evening Lubisch asked me to have dinner with him, and I enjoyed a rather delicious meal served with the best wine, obviously taken from the cellar at the Chateau. After eating, we enjoyed a pleasant conversation about our childhoods and families. Sigmund, he had asked me to call him by his Christian name when we were on our own, bent to pour me another drink and kissed me on the tip of my nose. I looked up at him, and he put the bottle down, lifted me up from the chair, and kissed me passionately. I kissed him back and as our tongues probed one another, his hand gradually moved up my leg until his fingers were slipping inside my silk panties.

He gently stroked me until I was silky wet (against all my willpower). He gradually slid my panties down, and I felt the softness of the silk around my ankles. All this time he had not stopped kissing me and picked me up and laid me on the couch. My skirt was expertly removed, and he sat up and looked appreciatively at my long legs encased in silk stockings and topped with lacy suspenders. He put my hand on his hardness and began again to stroke me, deliciously. I could feel myself rising towards a climax and held his hand to stop him. He removed his clothing and my blouse and bra.

Sigmund then started to stroke me and kiss and suck my nipples. I was virtually bursting with desire when he entered me. We moved in unison and quickly came to a united climax. I was shaking but sated with Sigmund still lying on top of me.

"That was wonderful, Nicole," Sigmund said huskily.

"For me too," I answered, ashamed that this Nazi could arouse such feelings in me.

"Let's go to your room, Nicole. There is no one about."

We bundled up our clothes and ran up the stairs to my room. As soon as we were there, Sigmund shut the door and gently pushed me onto the bed. He entered me as soon as we were horizontal and very slowly and expertly brought us both to an amazing climax. Shortly after, Sigmund dressed and left my room, leaving the door open.

"Thank you, *Liebling*. I have wanted you from the day you showed such a fighting spirit against Schultz and more so when I saw you in your nightdress in the middle of the road. Good night."

"Good night, Sigmund."

I went over and over what had just happened and could not condone in any way how I let myself be seduced, willingly, by a Nazi. In the morning I still felt ashamed. How could I? *Obviously, quite easily*, I thought.

I went to my office and got on with my tedious job. I would go home at lunchtime, sort out my house, and look for a new hiding place for my radio, but first, I would clean it up to get rid of the smell that seemed to permeate from the case.

When I arrived at the house, I knew someone had been there. I went into the yard and pretended to tidy up the pots and found what I was looking for: a message from Claude and another encrypted message that must be sent. The only way I could do this was to take the radio back to the Chateau and send the message from there in the hope that because so many messages went out from there, another would not be noticed.

I retrieved the radio, took it into the house, and cleaned it to get out the residual smell of the privy. I polished the case with shoe polish and poured perfume, or rather cheap cologne, over it. I found a suitcase in one of the cupboards and decided to wrap the radio in some sheets, then covered the sheets with clothing and put shoes on top. I left a message for Claude in the cellar, not a written one, but a sort of puzzle made up of pots, which was very basic. It said I was okay and that the message would be sent. We had a different message to let Claude know if I was in danger.

I left the house with my case and walked confidently back to the Chateau. I heard one or two gibes about my being a Nazi whore, but I pretended I was oblivious to them. I went straight up to my room, left the door open as instructed, sat on the side of the bed so that part of me could be seen if anyone should look up the stairs but, of course, not my hands. I had to read the encrypted message as I sent it; the tapping sound seemed to be so loud I was certain someone would hear it. Luckily no one did, and I packed up the radio and placed it on top of the compactum where it was hidden by the ornamental top that hid anything placed on top. I knew I had to get the radio away from here, but I just did not know how at the moment. I sat for quite a while, but no running soldiers came for me, which made me think I had managed to send the message without detection. I hoped whatever the message, it would save our brave soldiers who worked in such small groups.

I went back to my tedious work translating the files and came across evidence of corruption involving the mayor. I had no qualms reporting this as the individual concerned was helping the Nazis in any way he could, putting innocent people at risk.

I had been given the use of a bike, so after work, I cycled out into the countryside. Some members of my family, now deceased, had lived in a hamlet called le Maison Neuf consisting of just two or three houses, all of which were derelict. I thought this would be an ideal place for an imaginary resistance cell. I sorted it out to look as though it had been used recently by a cell and even dropped a small piece of a radio, redundant for any use on my radio. I hid it well so the Nazis would have to really search to find it. I had also dropped two or three cigarette butts that I had picked up in the streets, knowing they would be useful in the future.

When I returned to the Chateau, it was dark. I still did not have my papers, so there was a bit of a kerfuffle when I reached the gates of the Chateau while the soldiers phoned but could not reach Lubisch. Eventually Schultz came sauntering down to the gates and after holding a general conversation of no significance, told the soldiers that I was Lubisch's whore and to let me in. I cycled to the back of the Chateau, left my bike under cover, and went into the kitchen where a large German civilian was cooking dinner. Her name was Eva, and she was a very pleasant person. She smiled as I went in.

"Would you like a nice cup of coffee? It has just percolated and is one of the best we have?"

I thanked her and sat down at the large table to drink it. Schultz came in and sat down next to me, his fat thigh pushing against my leg. As he reached for the sugar, he squeezed my breast. I did not move. I knew Eva had seen this and a look of distaste passed across her face. I got up and thanked Eva for the coffee and went to my room. I had no intention of giving any information to Schultz and would wait for Lubisch to return. I was wracking my brain trying to decide where to keep the radio, so I couldn't relax. I had to have access to it on short notice, but using it at the Chateau again would be certain suicide.

Chapter 6

After we had congregated in the dining room for our evening meal, a quiet one for some reason, I went for a walk around the grounds to try to settle down. How I loathed Schultz. I knew I should feel the same way about Lubisch but I couldn't. He excited me and, to my shame, I looked forward to our next meeting.

To my horror as I walked across the lawn in darkness, I saw Maurice and Schultz in a jovial conversation, each holding a glass of wine and a cigarette. They looked completely at ease with each other. I had to inform Claude of this liaison as a matter of extreme urgency.

I had no option but to risk everything. If Maurice saw me I was dead, and if I did not contact Claude, most of the cell might be compromised. I ran to the treeline at the end of the lawn as faraway from the Chateau as I could get. I managed to get through the derelict fencing without too much effort and made my way towards my house. Claude's office or home, I did not know which, was on the outskirts of Blois in the opposite direction. I got there safely and, making sure there was no one around, I knocked lightly on the window. Claude immediately opened the door and dragged me in.

"What is it, Nicole?"

"I have just seen Maurice in a very cosy conversation with Major Schultz at the Chateau. They were drinking wine, smoking, and laughing as though they were long, lost friends.

If he sees me I am dead and so is the rest of the cell. I am sure Schultz would take extreme pleasure in wiping us all out, especially me."

I was gabbling, but I was worried not only for myself, but also for Pierre, Gerrard, Claude, and all those I did not know. I told Claude about the set up at le Maison Neuf, and we decided that once I told Lubisch what I found, I should lure Maurice there when they were going to search it.

"Have you a gun, Nicole?" Claude enquired.

"No, but if Maurice sees me he will surely let the Nazis know I am in the resistance, and they will capture me immediately. He obviously has their confidence, and they will believe whatever he tells them. I know I am Lubisch's lover, but that would mean nothing to him if he even suspected me of double-dealing."

"I understand all that, but we have no choice. One of us has to kill Maurice whenever and wherever we see him. Here is a small handgun that you can hide discreetly about your person in case you get the opportunity to kill Maurice before he kills you and the rest of us. The same applies to us all."

"Oh, I certainly will with pleasure if he does not get me first. Schultz hates me and would be yet another problem if they were together when and if I found Maurice. Listen, Claude, you will have to change your address as I may have compromised this one, although I am certain no one followed me. I am also going to stay at my house tonight. Schultz, yet again, made a pass at me, and I will tell Lubisch that I was frightened and did not want to stay at the Chateau whilst he was away."

"I will take you back to your house by a completely different route, Nicole. Thank you for your bravery; you have already saved many lives. Unfortunately, I am unable to tell you any details."

"Thanks, Claude, the less I know the better."

True to his word Claude took me back to my little house by a completely different route, one I must remember, and I was soon tucked up in my own bed, with the doors unlocked as usual. I slept fitfully. When I woke really early in the morning, I washed and dressed. Because I had no fresh food in the house, I made my way back to the Chateau. I now had the added fear that Maurice would see me and give me away.

I went straight into the kitchen where Eva was already baking. "Could I have a cup of coffee and a piece of bread please, Eva?"

"Of course you can, but where have you been."

"I slept at my own house because I was afraid Schultz was going to assault me again. You saw him when he sat next to me at the table yesterday. He really gives me the creeps."

"But if you are caught outside the Chateau at night it could have unpleasant consequences for you. Lubisch is a very hard man and intent on furthering his career. I doubt he is capable of real affection."

I did not reply to this but I was sure that he did feel affection for me, or maybe he was just seeking sexual gratification and I happened to be the best thing available at the time. I felt quite disgusted with myself when I realised that I was longing to be in his arms.

Chapter 7

Although 17 May was a Saturday, I resumed my boring work. I had just started translating another file from the Marie when Lubisch sent for me. I was really looking forward to seeing him, and my shame seemed to be of little consequence to me. When I entered his office, he had his back to me, but when he turned, I was drawn into the depth of his wonderful blue eyes and impressed by his striking physique.

"Where were you last night, Nicole?"

"I went to my house, Sigmund. Schultz was going to take his chance with you being away, and I was frightened. He touched me sexually whilst we sat at the kitchen table. Eva was witness to it."

"Well you are not my personal property. Others are going to try to seduce you." I could not believe what Sigmund had just said. It was cutting and meant to put me in my place. "In the future you are not allowed to leave the Chateau without permission, is that clear?"

"Of course," I said, tears welling in my eyes.

Sigmund turned his back to me and again looked out of the window. "What did you find out on your little cycling trip yesterday?"

"Actually, I am pretty certain that I found a place that is used by either the resistance or some other pro-French group. It is a little hamlet called la Maison Neuf, consisting of only two or three derelict buildings, but there was definite evidence that it had been used as some sort of gathering." I felt the pride in my voice whilst I was relating my imaginary find.

"Can you direct my troops there?"

"Of course, any time you wish," I said confidently, my emotions now under control.

"Very well. At dawn tomorrow you can lead us to la Maison Neuf. I hope it is going to be worthwhile." As he said these words, he turned to look at me and had what I thought was a slightly mocking look. "Off you go, then, and get on with your work. Perhaps you will come up with something useful today."

I could not resist saying, annoyed at his attitude, that I had, in fact, found monetary corruption within the Marie from the file I was translating and that if my work was of no use, I would be quite happy to go back to my house and try to find another job. My face was red and my eyes blazing as I tried to control my temper. He had deliberately implied that I was an easy lay and of little use to his cause. He obviously enjoyed my discomfort.

Sunday, 18 May, I was up and dressed at dawn and in the kitchen having a strong "wake me up" coffee. My little gun was tucked into the back of my trousers, covered by a long overcoat. I was banking on Schultz having told Maurice about my find and Maurice assuming that the woman Schultz referred to was me. He would be looking forward to turning me in.

Two truckloads of troops turned up, and one of the soldiers told me to get into the truck. Neither Lubisch nor Schultz were there in the trucks, and I assumed they would be coming in their Citroen. I directed the driver of the leading truck directly to la Maison Neuf. All the troops alighted and started a thorough search of the area. Unfortunately, I caught a glimpse of Maurice on the outskirts of the hamlet. I ducked down and crept, bent low, to where he was standing smoking a cigarette.

I got out my gun and said clearly but quietly, "Maurice."

As he turned towards me, I shot him in the head. I let out a scream and smashed his hand with a large piece of flint, fortuitously on the ground near me, and dropped the gun near me. The soldiers came running and I started my performance, crying hysterically and telling them between sobs that he was going to kill me and how I managed to knock the gun from his hand with the flint, pick up the gun, and shoot him.

"Oh God, is he dead? Poor man, what have I done? Why was he trying to kill me?"

All this was gabbled between breaks of inconsolable sobs while my nose ran and tears streamed down my face. What a performance! I needed desperately to know that he was dead to protect my identity but made out it was concern for this unknown man. Eventually one of the soldiers, obviously a medic, pronounced his demise. My relief nearly made me forget my act, but I managed to continue to cry, rubbing my eyes hard to make them as red as I could.

"How on Earth did you manage to get the gun away from the man?" asked one of the soldiers suspiciously.

"I hit his hand with that large flint as hard as I could. I am lucky that he did not shoot me straight away." I hiccupped and cried.

"It certainly seems that you were very lucky. That was some blow you dealt to his hand; most of the bones are probably broken. Did he already have the gun in his hand when he saw you?" the soldier continued, determined to get the most information he could.

"I am not quite sure; it all seemed to happen so fast. I think he already had it in his hand. Do you think he is a member of the resistance?" I cried some more. "Poor man. I have never hurt, let alone killed anyone before. I feel terrible."

A large black Citroen drew up and Lubisch and Schultz got out. "What have we got here?" asked Lubisch without glancing my way.

"Sir, this woman, who was showing us the whereabouts of a suspected meeting place of the resistance, has shot this man. Apparently he came at her holding a gun, which she knocked out of his hand with this large flint. You can see the damage to his hand. She must have some strength to do that much damage with one blow. She seems completely distraught," reported the private.

A shout came from a group of soldiers searching one of the derelict buildings. "Sir, we've found a piece of what probably came from a radio and also some cigarette butts."

Lubisch and Schultz marched over and examined the soldier's find. "Well done," said Lubisch. "It seems we have had a successful day." With that he got back into his car with Schultz and drove off.

"What are we going to do with the body?" I asked the private.

"Leave it here for his colleagues to find. It may warn them enough to leave the area, but we will be keeping a close eye out around here in case we come across more of the cell. They are not bright people, and some of them may come to get his body. He has no identification on him, but his clothes are definitely French."

How wrong you are, I thought. *The members of the resistance that I know are all exceptionally bright and brave, to risk all for their country.*

It was beginning to get quite chilly and when we drove back to the Chateau, sitting in the back of the open troop truck, I was shivering quite violently, not an act, but probably caused by my killing Maurice and the dramatics that followed. I was surprised that Lubisch did not speak to me, since most of the troops were aware that I was his moll. He had nothing to hide, but, of course, his high rank probably meant that he kept his private and professional lives completely separate.

On arrival back at the Chateau, Lubisch sent for me. "Well, well, Nicole, haven't you done well. Long may it last; I am sorry I have been short with you over the past few days, but things are moving quickly, and I expect to be moving on quite soon."

He moved towards me and put his arms around me, looked down into my eyes, mesmerising me like a rabbit "caught" in the headlights of a car. He bent down, cupped my face in his hands, and kissed me tenderly.

"I am afraid I cannot tell you where I am going, but you will always be on my mind. May I come to your room tonight?"

"Of course, Sigmund, I look forward to it."

"I must get on. Well done, Nicole, you have done very well."

I knew this was a dismissal and I turned, left his office, and made my way back to my office. As I was going along the corridor, I heard one of the other officers having a conversation on the phone, with the door open.

"So they have started rounding up the Jews in Lithuania as well as Germany. How are the railways managing to cope with the vast numbers?" He laughed heartily. "Squashed like sardines, eh! Well, hopefully, we might not have so many to gas when they arrive if the journey is made as bad as possible. I suppose they are still clutching their little cases of belongings as if that will make any difference to their fate, poor fools. They follow each other like sheep."

I heard him put the phone down and chuckle to himself, the cruel bastard. This was a vital piece of information I had to get to Claude. We all had Jewish friends, and they would soon be rounding up French Jews. I would have to use the radio once more inside the Chateau. I had no choice.

After I finished work for the day, again, nothing interesting found in the files, I went to my room. There was a lot of coming and going, so I hoped everyone would be too busy to pick up my short message. I retrieved the radio from the top of the compactum, positioned myself so that part of me could be seen from the bottom of the small staircase, and sent the message. I returned the radio to the top of the compactum just as I heard Sigmund coming up the few stairs.

He entered my room and closed the door. He came over to me and put his hand round the back of my neck. My heart leapt. Did he know I had just sent a radio message? I knew I had no need to worry when he pulled me to him, lowered his hands to my waist, and pulled me against him, so I could feel his hardness. He raised his right hand and started undoing the back of my blouse whilst the left hand undid my skirt, which fell to the floor. He then used both hands to remove my blouse and bra. He lowered his head and started kissing my breasts, sucking my nipples, and flicking them with his tongue, which caused a lovely sensation. We then just kissed as he gradually removed his clothes, helped by me. Sigmund was completely naked, his beautiful body glistening with sweat and his penis seemingly huge. I was just left in stockings and suspenders and Sigmund asked me to leave them on. He sat down on a narrow, armless chair and placed my legs on either side of his; then he sat me on his lap, entering me as he did so. He kissed and licked my nipples and gently gyrated himself inside me.

"Stop, Sigmund, please, I am nearly exploding."

"Me too, *Liebling*."

I got off his lap and we lay on my bed. He turned me over and rode me, doggy style, until we both exploded, again in unison. We were so well suited sexually, a Nazi and a resistance member, which seemed impossible. Although I was there to get as much gen on the Nazis as I could by any means, I still felt ashamed that I loved our lovemaking so much—yearned for it, in fact, when I didn't see Sigmund for a while.

As we lay back on the bed, we heard footsteps coming up the stairs and Schultz calling, "Lubisch."

"Okay, Schulz, I will be with you shortly."

Sigmund dressed quickly and still managed to look immaculate and cool even after our fiery session. He kissed me, properly, and then left without a word.

The following morning, I was absolutely starving and worried that Claude may not have received my message. I went down to the kitchen where Eva was sitting at the table. Troops were running everywhere, and the black Citroens were leaving the Chateau together with troop trucks. Something big was going on. I prayed it was not the start of rounding up Jews.

"Would you like something to eat, Nicole?"

"Yes please, I'm starving."

"I expect you are," said Eva smiling knowingly. We both sat down to a bowl of hearty soup full of vegetables and meat.

"Everyone seems to be running round like headless chickens," I said.

"There is a panic at the submarine base at La Rochelle. It seems there was an attack on it last night by the resistance."

I hid my joy and hoped that nobody had been hurt or captured. I again thought about my radio and decided that I really should move it whilst all the commotion was going on. I got it from my room and put it into the basket on my bike, making sure it was well covered. I started to ride out but decided to ask Eva if she needed any provisions whilst I was riding round.

"No thanks," she said. "All the provisions are delivered from the same source and as it is a Sunday, I don't think any stalls or shops will be open. I think they are afraid that an attempt might be made to poison them if they purchase food from the locals!"

Off I cycled singing light-heartedly to cover my fear that I would be discovered with the radio. Where I was going to hide it I did not know, but I had to find somewhere fast. I thought that I would have to go to my home and hide it somewhere near the railway bank so others could get access to it. I cycled home, knowing Sigmund had forbidden me to go there without permission.

Sigmund

There was nobody about, so I slid down the railway bank, waited to make sure all was clear, then went across the lines and into the woods. I knew there was a wrecked tractor there, and I could leave the radio tucked up above the wheel arch and under the rusted mudguards. Of course, I had to send Claude a message to say where I had hidden it. After I had done this, I scrambled up the bank and into my yard. I could still not detect any sign of life. I went inside and washed and changed and then cycled back to the Chateau. Before I did so, I thought it prudent to have a reason for going home, so I picked up a box containing some lovely cufflinks belonging to my father that I had come across whilst cleaning out some drawers. I knew that he had never used them or even liked them; typical of his age and upbringing, he felt that ornate jewellery was for women. They were small, neat, and classy—sapphires set in oblongs of gold. I knew Sigmund would love them.

On my way back I saw Claude, and he gestured that I sit on the grassy bank not far from the Chateau. He had positioned himself somewhere behind me under cover but, as he instructed, I never turned or let on someone was talking to me.

"Do not answer me or speak to me as they may be watching you," Claude said. "Well done in dealing with Maurice. He has caused the death of two of our operatives. Thank you, too, for telling us about the Jews in Lithuania being rounded up. You have proved yourself brave, intelligent, and loyal, and I think you should have a break, not only for your own safety but also for ours. Jews are being rounded up in Germany, Poland, and France. We believe they are being exterminated, and we are trying to get a line of escape set up as soon as we can. In the meantime, please warn all the Jews you know to get out.

"I saw where you hid the radio and also got your message. You must be more careful not to be seen, Nicole; I saw you quite easily. We have an escaped Jewish family in your cellar at the moment. They were hiding there when you went back, so I really believe we can use this as a hiding place for some time since you did not see anything untoward. The biggest problem is Blanche; as you say, we worry about her loyalty. We will move them as soon as we can, but don't go home again until we have contacted you further, and definitely don't try any unnecessary bravery!"

Those were Claude's last words before he left. I did not turn or change my stance in any way. After about ten minutes I got up, stretched, and cycled to the Chateau. It was obvious that my time as radio operator was at an end. I would now have to concentrate on saving as many Jewish families as I could.

I went straight to my room, tidied myself up, and then went back to the tedium of my allotted employment. How long I could stand this boredom I did not know, but I was sent to France to fight and I intended to do that through hell or high water. I did not work long as it was Sunday and not a compulsory workday. I was getting peckish and wondered if Eva had made apple strudels as she had promised. When I entered the kitchen, I had my answer: the smell was mouth-watering. Eva smiled broadly as she placed a plate in front of me with two strudels.

For the next week I carried on with my work, actually finding an official document that listed possible German collaborators; one of which was the mayor. This was probably why he was so sure of himself whilst in the company of the SS.

How I was going to let the resistance know without a radio I did not know, but I was pretty sure that there was an ally in the bakers. I had no choice but to risk finding out if this was, indeed, the case as my findings in the files could actually lead to the SS discovering and arresting members of the resistance. The mayor was always in contact with the local villagers and could glean useful information from people: Blanche for instance. The mayor actually gave the persona of putting people at ease, and they could easily be enticed into giving information that they thought would help the village. I put this particular file at the bottom of the pile as though I had not already translated it. I had not seen Sigmund at all, but he did send a note to say he hoped to be back soon.

Chapter 8

On 26 May, I went to the bakers where I thought an ally of the resistance worked, but I had no idea who it might be. My only hope was that the person knew me. I went into the bakers where a large woman was standing behind the counter, surrounded by the delicious aroma of freshly baked bread purveying throughout the shop. I looked at all the bread but did not select a loaf.

"Can I help you?" the large woman asked.

"I just cannot make up my mind, they all look delicious," I said, sounding a bit feeble; after all it was only bread!

The woman went to the back of the shop into what I assumed to be the living quarters. Shortly after, a middle-aged, rather haggard man came into the shop from the back. He stood and looked at me as if daring me to speak. Instead it was he who spoke.

"Nicole?"

At least he knew who I was.

"Yes, I am Nicole. I don't know if I would like any of this bread. I have discovered some of the loaves are not what they appear to be."

"All bread in this shop is made by me, and only me. I have no other employees. The woman you have already met behind the counter is my wife."

"I have discovered some who seem to be more to the Germans' taste than ours," I replied.

I decided I had to trust my own judgement, and I handed the man the list of names. He rewarded me with a lovely fresh loaf, and I left the shop just as a couple of women came in, one of which was Blanche.

"Hello, Blanche, how are you?"

Blanche did not answer but turned to her companion and said, "That's the German's whore who used to live next to me. Her poor parents."

I did not wait to hear anything else. I made my way back to the Chateau, hoping and praying that this was the man who would get the list to the resistance. I nearly laughed when I thought of the conversation I had with the baker, a very childish attempt to ascertain whether he was pro-resistance or not. Actually, I was sure he was, and I hoped the German collaborators would be dealt with or at least the whole resistance would be told of their disloyalty to France and her allies. I would have to wrack my brain for more plausible cover stories in the future, as I would have other lives to keep safe as well as my own.

Two days later, 28 May, I heard through the grapevine that a few Frenchmen had been found shot, but not by the Germans. Obviously Schultz was concerned that there was a spy working in their midst. Schultz had told another SS officer that the source had been pretty useful to them—letting them know of infiltrators, escaped prisoners of war, the whereabouts of Jews, and more. He and the other SS officer discussed whether or not to get rid of the rest of the men working for them to alleviate any more information leaks.

"I think we should wait for Lubisch to come back before we take matters further, but we certainly must not have loose talk when they come to make their reports. I have my doubts about the accounts clerk, Schultz, so we must only talk trivia whilst the French are here," said the SS officer, whose name I did not know.

It would seem that they did not suspect me, at least not at this time. I decided I had to get rid of the file in which the names were listed, and I wondered why the mayor would keep such a list.

I got back to the Chateau and gave Eva the bread.

"Thanks, Nicole. Sigmund arrived back about half an hour ago. He looks completely washed out."

"Did he ask for me?"

"No. He went straight to his office and shut the door. I think he locked it."

I went to my own office, got on with my work, and tried not to think of Sigmund or the list that I hoped I had given to the right man. The day dragged, but at last it was time for us to have dinner. When I went to freshen up for dinner, I took the file with me and hid it under my mattress. I would burn it as soon as I had the opportunity. Sigmund did not join us for repast, but nobody mentioned his absence. Schultz was ogling as usual, but I tried to ignore him, which was not really hard with much more serious things on my mind. After dinner I plucked up courage to go to Sigmund's office and knocked at the door.

"Come in."

I opened the door and went over to his desk. He looked dreadful: white, and haggard.

"Sigmund, what on earth is the matter? You look dreadful."

"Hello, *Liebling*. I have just come back from a most horrific visit to Warsaw in Poland. I can't say anything further, but I need to be in your arms as soon as I can."

"I am going to my room now, Sigmund. Come as soon as you wish." I had hardly had time to titivate myself a little when he arrived, taking me into his arms and holding me as tightly as he could.

"Nicole, I have missed you so much. I know I should not get involved with you, but I really can't help it."

We started kissing passionately and removing each other's clothes. As we lay down on the bed, it was obvious that Sigmund was not in a fit state for lovemaking.

Sigmund clung to me as he whispered, "I'm sorry, Nicole, so sorry."

"Don't be silly, Sigmund, it really does not matter. Just hold me."

As we lay in each other's arms, I was sure I could feel his wet tears trickling between my breasts, but I made no mention of this. We fell asleep in each other's arms but spent a restless night as Sigmund was troubled and upset. He tossed and turned when he was actually sleeping and when awake just stared into space. I wondered what happened to him in Poland. In the morning Sigmund seemed to be his usual self, but whether this was an act I was not sure. He still looked pale, and his beautiful blue eyes appeared troubled. He kissed me good-bye and said he would see me this evening.

I was desperate to help the Jews escape and decided that I would go back to my house despite Claude's warnings and the fact that I was supposed to get permission from Sigmund. I went to my office and half-heartedly got on with translating the files. I had put the offending file in my bag before leaving my room.

The day dragged, but at 4:00 p.m. I set off and got to my house without being stopped. Sigmund had still not returned my papers. I went into the house using the front door, which was unlocked as usual. Everything seemed exactly as I had left it. My first task was to put the file in the range and set fire to it, making sure that every piece of the file was destroyed.

I went into the backyard, checked to see that Blanche was not in her yard, and entered the basement where I found three people: a woman, and two children. I reassured them that there was nothing to fear and that I would do my best to help them. I asked them how long they had been there, and the woman said this was their fourth day, and she was hopeful that they would be getting out that evening. I decided there and then that I would stay with them until Claude, or whoever was going to move them, came. I would insist on helping them escape.

We held our conversations in whispers in case anyone came into the yard. The woman, who was Jewish and did not wish to tell me her name, told me that they had been captured by the SS and were taken to a holding centre, overflowing with Jewish prisoners. The holding centre was in the railway sidings somewhere on the French and German borders. Each day cattle trucks arrived and people were packed into the trucks liked sardines. Little children were unable to breathe unless someone picked them up so they were level with the rest of the prisoners and could get air, as putrid as it was.

The woman said that someone grabbed her and her girls, and they were somehow pushed into the nearby undergrowth and taken to a place of apparent safety. They were moved several times before they actually got to my house, but tonight they were to be flown out, possibly to England. I told the woman that this was my house but that I was not a resistance member. I told her that if at all possible I would be able to help them escape. Eventually Claude arrived. He was amazed and cross that I was there.

"What on Earth are you doing?" he asked, avoiding the mention of my name.

"I have come to help. I am fed up doing nothing when there is so much to be done. I can take these people to their pickup area and free you up to get more to safety."

"I don't know what I am going to do with you, but we certainly need help. Can you take them to the outskirts of La Boussier en Gatin, the field to the left of the church?"

"Of course. When?"

"Right now. I will make sure there is no one close by, but then you will be on your own."

Claude got out through the trapdoor and beckoned us to follow him after a few minutes. We all wriggled out, went to the edge of the yard, and down the bank. I knew my way to the pickup point and knew we would be able to stay under cover most of the way without coming across German patrols. Luck was on our side, and I got the woman and the two terrified children to the pickup point.

I waited as three men guided a small plane in with flares and lifted the three escapees onto the plane. Finally, I watched the plane take off safely. We all dashed for cover and waited a while to make sure our operation had not been seen. Each of us went our separate ways without one word being spoken. Of course, I had no idea where the family was going but hoped that wherever they ended up, they would be safe and have a good life.

Uneventfully I got back to my house, went in through the front door, changed into my nightclothes as though I had just gotten up and crumpled the bedclothes, and although it was already dawn, put the light on. I busied myself pretending to tidy up, hoping that anyone about would think I had spent the night there. I went back to the Chateau at 9:00 a.m. and asked to see Sigmund. Eventually I was summoned to his office. When I got there, his office was empty, so I sat down opposite his desk. I had not been there long when Schultz came in. He started when he saw me, turned, and went back out. I had a feeling he was up to something but could not even hazard a guess as to what it could be. After about half an hour Sigmund had still not arrived, so I went to my office and reluctantly translated yet more rubbish. After lunch Sigmund actually came to my office and enquired what I needed to see him about.

"Sigmund, my identification papers have still not been returned."

"I'm sorry, Nicole, I had forgotten I still had them. Come with me, and I will return them to you."

When we got to his office, he went to a locked cupboard, sorted through some papers, and handed me my documents.

"Are you intending to go somewhere, Nicole?"

"Not immediately, but I might want to have a break whilst it seems reasonably peaceful. Don't know if I should mention this, but when I was waiting in your office this morning Schultz came in. He seemed surprised that anyone was there and left quickly. I thought he acted somewhat suspiciously, but I know it is none of my business."

"No, it isn't, but it is my business to ask you where you were last night," Sigmund said, staring into my eyes.

"I went to my home to get something and decided to stay the night in case I got stopped without papers." I put my hand in my pocket and took out the lovely little blue leather box and handed it to him. "I thought you needed cheering up, Sigmund, and thought you would like these. They belonged to my father."

Sigmund opened the box and smiled at me. "They are lovely. What a kind gesture, *Liebling*." He took me in his arms and kissed me passionately. "Was that the only reason you went home, I wonder?" These were Sigmund's dismissive words as he picked up the phone and waved me out his office.

After leaving his office, I remembered I had not told him that I wished to return to my home to live, but that was what I was determined to do whether he liked it or not. There were hundreds of Jews and other escapees that needed help, and Claude had little enough men without me leaving the group. So that evening after work I went home, taking some provisions that Eva had given me, with a strong warning about the wrath of Lubisch and Schultz. I was not worried about Sigmund, but I was worried about Schultz, who would dearly love to see me come to harm.

Sigmund did not arrive at my house that night as expected, and I did not see him when I went to work the following day or the next. Saturday, 2 June 1941. I asked Eva if she had seen him.

"I think he has been sent to organise a mission in Poland or Germany, but I have no idea if this is permanent."

"I suppose Schultz is still here?" I asked sullenly.

"I am afraid so, dearie."

When I got home that afternoon, I decided to tidy up the yard and make sure there were no tell-tale signs that the trapdoor had been used or left unhidden. Of course all was well. Claude and the others were so dedicated and brave and would have made certain of this. Claude actually turned up that evening and asked if I could go with him, to take a whole set of clothing for someone trying to get away from being sent to the work camps.

"Of course I will," I said without even thinking about it.

I rustled up clothing and shoes and tied them in a roll so that I could put them under my armpit with a strap over my shoulder to assist me whilst clambering around wherever we were going. Claude did not inform me of our destination but led the way with extreme caution. We had to hide several times, unnecessarily most of the time, but we were once within the sound of a German patrol whispering and had to lay low for at least half an hour. After this, we went into much heavier cover, which was marshy underfoot and made going very slow as my stupid shoes, slip-ons, kept getting left behind in the mud when I lifted my feet.

Eventfully we arrived at a small house near Samur where we found two pathetic specimens of human life: a man and woman, gaunt and haunted looking. My clothing, although small, hung on the poor woman's painfully thin body. Their story was incredible. Both were doctors and had been used by the SS to carry out diabolical pain-inflicting torture to make their victims admit to being Jewish. When they refused, they were slung into a barn with many others with hardly any room to move. There was a bucket in one corner for, men, women, and children to defecate and the stench was horrendous. They were fed only dry bread occasionally and given a large bucket of water to be shared sparingly amongst them all. Many were sick, especially the elderly and very young.

The SS apparently stole many of their valuables and kicked and beat them for no apparent reason. The two doctors were ordered to remove gold teeth from the Jews, and when they said they had no instruments to carry out such procedures, a pair of filthy pliers was produced for them to use.

Nobody had any inclination to try to escape, probably because they were weak and worried about their families and what retribution would be handed out to them if they did. Our two wards were still fairly strong and able to escape but they really couldn't recall how, saying they just made a dash for it. This worried the resistance. Had the couple been allowed to escape, to root out the underground movement helping prisoners to escape?

They were kept hidden for a couple of weeks with no sign that they could be stooges, something that was on our minds continually as we knew the Germans were devious and the story of the couple's escape seemed unrealistic, but we had to take them at face value until we found out otherwise. Getting food was a problem, because resistance members could not risk going back and forth and being caught while waiting until it was time to move them permanently.

Claude asked if I was up to moving them to a derelict farm two miles from Samur where the last leg of their journey would be undertaken by boat that would take them to the south coast of England from a little cove near St Malo. Of course I was more than willing and just had to wait for the green light. I studied the maps of the area and pickup point until I knew the roads, paths, woods, and possible German billets by heart.

It was nerve wracking waiting to take the couple to their liberation, but on Thursday, 7 June, I was told that I had to get the Jews to the pickup site that night. I had a feeling of foreboding, which was uncharacteristic, but I could not shake it off. I studied the couple intently and made my plans to escape if they turned out to be imposters. Eventually we were told that it was time to get going and the three of us set off. Obviously, we had not shared our names as a safeguard.

The first section of the journey was slow because it was in a built-up area, and I had to make sure that there were no patrols. I still felt uneasy and did not want this couple to be able to find their way back to the safe house, so I decided to make several unnecessary diversions. After several detours, which were time consuming, we started the section of paths through woodland and scrub. We were absolutely silent and kept under cover. When I saw silhouettes of what were probably German soldiers in the distance, my worst fears were confirmed and I jumped, hoping the couple had not noticed.

"I must go to the loo, I am desperate. Wait here and keep absolutely quiet," I whispered, trying to act normally. "I won't be a minute."

These were the first words to come into my mind. I dashed deeper into the woodland and ran for my life. My legs and face were being scratched by the brambles and twigs as I made my way carefully back to the safe house, going virtually round and round in circles in order to make certain I was not being followed. When I entered the house, Claude could not hide his surprise.

"My, that was quick, Nicole."

"It was a trap, Claude. Luckily, I saw what I presumed to be either the SS or German soldiers in the distance and ran for my life. I have gone round in circles several times to make sure I was not followed. I took the couple on a wild-goose chase on the way to the pickup point, so they would not be able to direct the Germans here," I said, feeling rather proud of myself and relieved that I had returned to the safe house.

"Nevertheless, we must all get out of here now and not come back!" Claude said firmly.

Without more ado, we left to go our separate ways all wishing each other good luck. No one knew when we would next meet now that there was a worrying increase in SS tactics.

I got home in the daylight on 8 June. Unfortunately, my stockings were in tatters, and my legs and face quite badly scratched. However, I got home to find the house had been ransacked. I wondered if the Jews had given me away, but if they had, I was sure the house would have been searched before now. I decided to have a bath in the metal bath that was kept in the yard. I heated two buckets of water on the range that I had just lit and a couple of saucepans on the cooker as well. Once the water was at the right temperature, I added some bath salts that Sigmund had given me, and soon the lovely fresh smell of lavender filled the kitchen. I got into the bath, now aware of my aches and pains, and luxuriated in the soft water. I didn't realise I had dropped off until I awoke to Schultz grabbing my breasts.

"Oh, you are back. Where have you been? I thought you would like some company with Sigmund being away," said Schultz, virtually drooling at the sight of my naked body.

"You thought wrong then, didn't you? Don't you dare touch me, you filthy pig!" I screamed at him. With that he grabbed me by my hair and dragged me out of the bath.

"What did you say? Don't touch me? I will do what I like. You are just a French whore after all and certainly not Sigmund's personal plaything."

He was trying to kiss me and grabbing at my crotch with his fat fingers, which was proving painful. He managed to kiss me with his fat, wet lips whilst holding my arms behind my back with his other hand, and I thought I was going to vomit.

"Lie down," he said.

"I will not."

His answer was to push me with all his force to the floor whilst starting to remove his trousers. I was near the range and grabbed the iron poker lying next to it. I got to my feet as he was trying to get his fat, flabby legs out of his trousers while standing on one foot, and I smashed him with all my force across his head, which seemed to explode, shooting blood and tissue all over the place. Schultz was completely poleaxed and hit the floor, once again hitting his head on the edge of the range on his way down. I knew instinctively he was dead. What the hell was I going to do? There was no way I was strong enough to move his body very far, and the kitchen looked like an abattoir. Like with all the head wounds, there was so much blood.

I had no choice but to go back to the bakers. I cleaned up as much as I could. I cleaned the wall that was splattered with blood and got rid of the pool of blood, a very grisly job, all while the half-trousered body of Schultz lay there. I kept thinking he would get up. I covered him with the rug from my living room floor and pulled the kitchen table in front of the cadaver so that if anybody looked in the window, it would not be seen. In fact, no one had ever looked in the kitchen window that I did not know.

I realised that I was still naked and dashed upstairs to dress and tidy up my hair. I locked up when I left the house and made my way to the bakers, not far from the Chateau. I prayed that nobody who knew me would be about. I tried to walk as leisurely and carefree as I could and, apart from two German soldiers who recognized me from being in the company of their superior officer, Lubisch, and nodded to me, I saw no one else. I entered the bakers and was lucky enough to find the same gentleman whom I had previously handed the note containing the list of collaborators.

"I have no other way to say this, but I have killed an SS officer in my house. He is far too heavy and big for me to deal with, and I need help. I must tell you that he resides at the Chateau and will be missed quite quickly. He came to my house to rape me. I need help desperately but realise this is a very dangerous situation and whoever helps me, if they are willing to do so, will be at great risk." I gabbled the situation almost without taking a breath. The baker nodded.

"Just go home. Act as normal as possible and someone will contact you." After handing me a loaf, he went to the back of the shop and shut the door behind him.

I made my way home and let myself in, locking the door behind me. I went into the kitchen, emptied the bath, and dragged it back into the yard. I turned it over to completely empty it and saw Blanche in her yard.

"What's happened to your fancy man, then?" she asked sarcastically. "Dumped you, has he? No Frenchman will want you. You know that, don't you?" With that she went into her house and banged the door shut.

I did not want to be in the house and tried to find things to do in the yard. I cleaned all the windows, watered the pathetic looking shrubs that were in the pots, and then went back inside. I went upstairs, sat on my bed, and cried.

In the early hours of Saturday, 9 June, Claude, Gerrard, and another man arrived. I had remembered to leave the door unlocked.

"Well, Nicole, what have you done?" asked Claude putting his arms around me. I just pointed to the large mass on the floor. Claude removed the rug and started to laugh at the sight of Schultz lying there with one leg in his trousers and his buttocks and the other leg naked.

"He tried to rape me, Claude," I sobbed, due more to shock at the bloody result of my actions than anything else.

They wrapped Schultz in the rug, tied it round him tightly, and the three of them picked him up. They went to the edge of the yard and let the body roll down the railway bank. I followed and watched to make sure there was no one nearby. When they reached the track, they picked Schultz up and hurried along the railway tracts as fast as the heavy body allowed.

I returned inside and started searching for anything that may have dropped out of Schultz's pockets. I could find nothing. Next, I scrubbed the floor thoroughly. I had some whitewash in the cupboard and found an old brush and used them to whitewash the walls of the kitchen, which was so tiny that it only took a couple of hours to complete all exposed walls. I washed the curtains in case of blood splatter and put them in front of the range to dry. I waited for the commotion to start. The searching of houses and the arrest of people until they found out where Schultz had gone. I realised that people would be tortured and possibly shot because of Schultz's disappearance, but this was war and I had to keep that in mind. I wondered if Schultz had told anyone he was going to try his luck with me.

Chapter 9

Two days went by and nothing happened. There seemed to be fewer soldiers on the streets than normal and an air of uncertainty. I, of course, had no one to talk to, due to my fraternising with the enemy. None of the resistance members had contacted me, and I assumed that everyone would be lying low after the scare in Samur.

I tried to carry out mundane jobs around the house, read, and even sew, but I was so agitated I was unable to settle. I went for long walks, which I enjoyed as the sun was shining brightly and the seasonal plants and flowers were out in abundance. This helped to tire me so I could get a reasonable sleep, something I had found difficult since killing Schultz. Time passed slowly, and after two days there was still no one searching for Schultz.

The following morning, June 12, however, the soldiers started house-to-house enquiries asking if anyone had seen Schultz or knew of his whereabouts. Apparently he was going to Poitier to meet up with a friend, but had never arrived. When it was my turn, I put on my Oscar-winning act once again, and the soldiers went off without even searching my house or garden. Everyone else had been subjected to this, and I knew that tongues would wag again.

Several villagers were taken in for questioning but were released unharmed. When they left us alone, we assumed the search went to Poitier. Another week went by and Tuesday evening, 19 June, I was sitting in my living room trying to concentrate on a novel when the front door opened and Sigmund walked in, looking pale and gaunt, with no life shining in his wonderful blue eyes. I jumped up and rushed into his arms spontaneously, and we kissed passionately. My heart was racing with excitement and what I now knew to be love.

"Where have you been, Sigmund? You look ill and exhausted."

"Nicole, *Liebling*, I have missed you so much. I have seen things that nobody should witness or allow, but I cannot tell you anything about it. I need you to hold me tight and never let me go."

"Oh, Sigmund, I would love to have you in my arms forever. Is there nothing I can do to help?"

"Nothing that would be allowed by the SS," he said sorrowfully.

"Sigmund, the SS believe I am helping you all by spying on my countrymen."

Sigmund did not speak for quite a while but held me tightly in his arms and then bent his head and kissed my lips, forehead, and cheeks. He caressed my breasts gently and whispered that he loved me. Gradually he started to undress me and then him and we pressed our naked bodies together as our juices began rising. We went upstairs to bed and made beautifully slow and gratifying love, again both climaxing together and saying, "I love you" at the same time.

In the morning I got up first and made us coffee and bread, all I had in the house, which seemed like ambrosia to us. As we ate, we basked in the knowledge that we really and truly loved each other.

"Sigmund, can you not tell me what you have been through. You now know I love you. I have things that I could tell you about me that I should not, but I will to prove my love."

"Nicole, I have to go to the Chateau this morning to give a report on my findings over the past few weeks. One of Hitler's closest allies will be there. I must look smart and look well, otherwise they will doubt my loyalty. It is rumoured that a lawyer named Nicolous Halem planned to assassinate Hitler and everyone, of course, is under extra scrutiny. I definitely did not know him, or have any knowledge of him before this attempted assassination plot, but I did attend a Protestant monastery primary school in Robleden, Berlin where he also attended but not at the same time."

"You always look smart, Sigmund, and if they query your paleness you can pretend that you are sick with a cold or flu quite easily. There is absolutely no reason to be concerned about knowing this Halem, as I am sure Hitler's henchmen will have rooted out anyone who has had contact with him and would certainly not check pupils who attended a primary school that he attended years ago."

"*Liebling*, you have such a calming influence on me, well mentally anyway." At last I saw a sparkle in his beautiful eyes.

"I must be off, mustn't be late. I will see you later and hopefully bring you something nice to cook for our dinner if Eva is in a good mood. Good-bye, my darling."

We clung together for a few seconds and kissed lovingly, my heart pounding. I wondered what my handler back in Britain would think of me now, or Claude for that matter although he had experienced my loyalty and bravery. Sigmund did not get back until 9:00 p.m. Obviously Eva had been in a good mood, because he carried with him steak, cheese, potato pie, and her delicious strudel.

"Wow! Eva was pleased to see you. I hope you weren't too pleased to see her."

I laughed happily. Sigmund also produced a bottle of a very good red wine, and we had a beautiful meal. Needless to say, after clearing up, we were anxious to get to bed to make love perhaps more than once, in a most passionate and satisfying way. We really could not get enough of each other as we explored each other's bodies to find our most exotic intimate places.

"I want to marry you, Nicole," Sigmund spurted out as if he was frightened the whole sentence would not come out if he said it slowly. "Obviously after the war. I know we have not known each other long, but I have no doubt that I want you to be my wife. I adore you."

"I want to marry you too, Sigmund, but we have known each other for such a short time, and I have to tell you some extremely serious things before this would be possible. Although I love you with all my heart, I have to think of others as well. I told you I would tell you some of my secrets, and one is that I have to help people in any way I can whatever the consequences."

Sigmund looked deep into my eyes. "You may recall that when you went to your house to get those beautiful cufflinks, I asked if that was the only reason you had gone to your house. I knew you had been up to something. I noticed the scratches healing on your face and limbs were not something you would get routinely. I too want and need to help people but in great numbers, which requires the help of others who I have to trust implicitly with my life. Well, are you going to marry me? We will marry properly in a church with our families present if they survive the war."

"Yes, Sigmund, I will marry you when the war is over, but some of my actions might put you in danger of being thought disloyal to Hitler if I am caught."

"So be it," said Sigmund. "All I know for sure is that I love you and will protect you through thick and thin. I have to return to the hell hole called Auschwitz in Poland tomorrow and watch unmentionable cruelty. I have been fortunate in that I have not had to carry out atrocities. I am busying myself planning the construction of large work camps and a railway, so until I know who my allies are, I hope this remains the status quo."

"Oh, Sigmund, you must do the right thing, even if you save one person, it is the beginning of bigger things."

Hardly able to pull away from each other, we kissed goodbye, and Sigmund left for Poland on Thursday, 21 June. As he was leaving, he said, "Schultz has gone missing."

"Do they know where he went? Has he gone AWOL? He seemed like a coward to me."

"They think he is in the Poitier area helping the resistance with information about the submarine base at La Rochelle," said Sigmund, running back a few steps to kiss me again as his car arrived to take him back to hell.

Chapter 10

Sigmund had the company of a sergeant on the long journey back to Auschwitz. There was hardly any conversation. Sigmund was worried about Nicole carrying out dangerous operations. His heart swelled with pride at the thought of this beautiful, slender, slip of a girl risking her life to help others. *I must do something too*, he thought.

Auschwitz, Poland was chosen for the site of the concentration and extermination camp. Hermann Goering had ordered all Jews to be sent to a ghetto, and he gave their homes to German workers and their families. When Sigmund arrived, the camp was full of Polish nationals, Jews, Russian prisoners of war, homosexuals, Jehovah's Witnesses, and thousands of people of diverse nationalities. All were hardly fed and living in squalor. Sigmund realised that he must stress to those in charge of prisoners that to avoid infectious diseases and put the prisoners to work, they must be fed better. Auschwitz was one of the networks of Nazi concentration camps built and operated by the Third Reich in Polish areas annexed by Nazi Germany. It consisted of Auschwitz 1, the original camp, Auschwitz 11–Birkenau, a combination concentration and extermination camp, and Auschwitz-Monowitz, a camp to staff an IG factory.

Prisoners built this factory 1 April 1941 on the orders of Hermann Goering, to try to make synthetic rubber. The prisoners had to walk seven kilometres each way, but at least they were fairly safe unless they became ill. There were also forty-five satellite camps. He noticed even greater numbers of prisoners since he had last been there. Seeing the little children with their terribly thin bodies and haunted eyes especially broke his heart. They were all forced to wear uniforms, which resembled pyjamas, and even in June they were hardly warm enough.

When he went into the officers' quarters, he was ashamed of the comfort displayed and knew he would have sufficient food. He asked his sergeant to arrange for all senior members of the camp to meet in his office at 8:00 p.m. When they were all assembled, he brought up the question of the necessity to feed prisoners better if they wanted to get the best work out of them.

There were huffs and puffs from the majority and one commandant said callously, "If we got rid of the children and those unable to work, we would be able to feed the workers properly."

"What do you mean get rid of the children and the infirmed adults?" he asked heatedly.

"Sigmund's going soft, must be love," a lieutenant said and laughed without humour.

"Whilst I am in charge here, my word goes. From now on the prisoners' rations must be increased. Heavens above, even increasing their rations will not be sufficient nourishment for a human being. What is it? A couple of bowls of watery soup made from vegetable peelings and slices of stale bread and water. Wonderful! This order is to be implemented immediately."

With that Sigmund left them to take it in. He could tell from their demeanour that they did not agree with him and would probably take it out on the prisoners.

When Sigmund toured the camp, often discretely giving a few biscuits to some of the children, he found that grills were being inserted into the roof of the huts, again at the behest of Goering. Piping led to them from a large generating room from where poisonous gas would be transferred to holding areas referred to as shower rooms. The railway led right to the gates of the camp and beyond. Sigmund felt sick to his stomach imagining what might be about to happen, knowing that the plan was to start exterminating prisoners beginning September 1941.

Of course, Sigmund's attitude towards caring for the prisoners was not well received, and his peers seemed to treat them worse than ever. Whenever he was about, the majority of guards behaved in a humane way, but he knew that as soon as his back was turned things changed for the worse, much worse.

Sigmund longed to see Nicole and hoped that she was safe, but he also hoped that she was able to help at least a few people escape what would have been a terrible end. If only he could devise a plan to help prisoners escape, but sadists surrounded him, so he knew it would be impossible. How they could possibly sleep at night and carry on as normal he could not fathom.

On Monday, 2 July, Sigmund got his orders to go to the Ukraine to join those fighting in Operation Barbarossa (code name for the Nazi invasion of the Soviet Union). Hitler's persistent desire was to conquer the Soviet territories. The fighting was heavy and leaving vast numbers of casualties and fatalities, the majority on the Soviet side. Sigmund was in command of a battalion of dedicated Nazis, mainly young men loyal to Hitler.

The Ukraine was only a small part of the 2,000 kilometre front, but the fighting was fierce. Sigmund was fully occupied with the strategies of his particular battalion and, of course, he was fighting for his country. Still, he could not get rid of the feeling that Hitler needed to be eliminated. He knew there had been several unsuccessful attempts to assassinate Hitler and was certain there were like-minded officers that wished for Hitler's downfall.

Sigmund learned from his fellow officers that German forces had captured over three million Soviet prisoners who apparently were not granted the protection stipulated in the Geneva Convention. Many knew of Hitler's "Hunger Plan," a program that would reduce the Eastern European population; Soviet prisoners were deliberately being starved to death.

Sigmund's spirits were low, but he was loyal to his troops and protected them with his brilliant strategies. He listened to their worries about the outcome of this operation and, of course, concerns about their loved ones. He was hugely respected by his troops.

Chapter 11

I settled back in a routine of being ignored by my fellow countrymen who were now in no doubt of my fraternisation with the Nazis. Sigmund and I had not hidden our closeness.

On Friday, 22 June, the Nazis started to search for Schultz in the village. About twenty people were arrested and taken to the Chateau, and I was one of them. There were also two local gendarmes, which I found strange because all they did was maintain the curfew and keep the roads clear for Nazis' cars to speed along. They were young and had probably just finished their training when war broke out. We were kept in a semi-dark, damp cellar, which was cold even though it was summer.

"Where is your lover now, Nicole?" said Gilbert, one of the shopkeepers in the town. I did not answer and just squatted against the wall, as there were no chairs or any other comforts whatsoever. We were kept there overnight and told that our homes would be searched once again. I plucked up courage to ask why we were being kept as prisoners. All I got was a withering look from our captor and a push with the butt of his gun. My fellow prisoners found this amusing, as did the soldier.

The following morning we were taken individually for interrogation. I think I was the fifth prisoner questioned, but I am not sure. My interrogation was not a pleasant experience, and they asked me time and again where Schultz was. My answer was always the same.

"I don't know where he has gone. I was not his confidant and only knew him in passing, apart from one episode when he sexually assaulted me without any provocation whatsoever."

My interrogator immediately picked up on this. "So you had reason to dislike Schultz, possibly even hate him," SS-Officer, Major Sturmbannführer Muller stated as if this was fact.

"I had no feelings apart from disgust for the man," I answered.

"So you did know him. Where is he?" There was a distinctive threat in the SS officer's voice.

"I did not know the man. I knew who he was because, as I have already told you, he sexually assaulted me when I worked at the Chateau translating the files from the Marie."

SS-Sturmbannführer Muller turned to speak to the other SS officer, not grasping the fact that as a translator of their files, I understood German, and told him to send me back to the cellar. I was pretty sure this would not be the last time I would see this man.

I was frog-marched back to the cellar and pushed inside. None of the other prisoners asked me anything, even Blanche, who usually was unable to contain her curiosity. All the prisoners were eventually interviewed and it must have been in the middle of the night when the interviews finished. Everybody was hungry and there was only a large jug of water, which everyone had to drink from. A bucket in the corner was provided as a latrine, which was overflowing. Someone called one of the guards to tell him, and without a second thought, he emptied it on the floor around us and left, wearing a vicious grin on his face. The stench was awful.

Sigmund

A few hours later several names were called, and these prisoners left the cellar. We still had no food, and I called to the guard in German that we needed food. There was no response. The prisoners who had been called did not come back, and because there was no activity in the yard, we assumed they had been allowed to go home. My fellow prisoners discussed this amongst themselves and surmised that after their houses were searched, they would be allowed to leave.

The two gendarmes guarding us were removed, and after a while we heard a kafuffle in the yard and the sound of marching boots. There was a lot of shouting, so I was unable to hear the conversations, but I did hear the word "fire" followed immediately by gunshots. I must try to remember the dates of these happenings, so I can report them to the authorities when the war is over. It was 24 June 1941, and I was certain that the two gendarmes were the ones executed. Claude once told me that given the chance, all Nazis loved to execute gendarmes.

A few hours later, seven more villagers were taken out of the cellar including Gilbert and Blanche, and there was no subsequent noise in the yard or gunshots. Hopefully, they had been allowed to go home. Another day passed without food, but early the next morning, 25 June, the door opened and a bucket containing bread and one with water were pushed in.

Fourteen prisoners had now been allowed to go, but two others had definitely been executed. The six that were left conversed in whispers, and most of the conversations were about our fate. Everyone was scared. We had not eaten or washed for days; we were dirty, smelly, and hungry. We didn't have the luxury of toilet paper, and we all had diarrhoea because of the filth left on the floor by the guards who had emptied the latrine bucket on the floor. Nobody was called that day and we spent another cold and sleepless night.

The next day, 26 June, we were all called out. I was taken to the office of Major Muller, who grimaced at my stench.

"Lucky for you we have found nothing in your home to implicate you with Schultz, and I have checked that you translated the files you informed me about. I also found out that you are willing to turn your own countrymen in to us and have helped us to find the location of one of the resistance's radio transmitting sites, even shooting one of the resistance members. Very commendable! I hope we will be able to call upon you again. You may now go, and for God's sake have a bath. You stink!"

"Thank you," I said sheepishly and thought, *I could just put a bullet through your smug face.*

It was dark when I arrived home. I lit the range and put buckets of water on to heat, which would not take long as I stacked the range with dry wood. I dragged the bath in the kitchen, stripped off my stinking clothes, and found fresh ones to put on after my bath. I put some lavender salts into the bath, which brought tears to my eyes when I thought of Sigmund. Fortunately, I had just wrapped an old blanket round me when Claude appeared in the kitchen.

"Are you all right, Nicole?" he asked caringly.

"Yes, apart from smelling like a latrine, being filthy dirty, and having been deprived of food. I was interrogated more than once, but when they realised that I had been "helping" them, their attitude seemed to change. They executed two young gendarmes for no apparent reason."

"This is one of their 'sports,'" said Claude.

"When will you need my help again? I must do something while Sigmund is away. He told me he has been seeing acts of unbelievable cruelty. I must tell you that he and I are in love, but we both want to do something to help save as many as we can but, of course, in different ways. He does not know what I have done, and I have no idea what he does. All I know is that he felt he was returning to hell when he left and looked quite distraught."

"I have two Jewish families to hide. Do you think you can take one family? It is very dangerous as you are obviously under scrutiny, but I have no one else I can rely on. Sadly, Pierre was caught and executed, poor boy. He gave nothing away even though he was tortured beyond what any human being could be expected to tolerate."

"Oh, poor Pierre, he was so young and so brave. His poor mother, she must be completely heartbroken. I can, of course, take a family. I will make the cellar more comfortable with a mattress and blankets. I have a reasonable supply of tin food from the Chateau. Do you think I should open the entrance from inside, the one that was blocked up?" My adrenaline was rising with the thought of being able to do something to thwart the Nazis.

"No, it is safer if the entrance is just the small trapdoor accessible from the yard only. Altering anything might alert the authorities. Anyway, I will let you have your much-needed bath." Claude laughed and wrinkled his nose. "Good night and

God bless, Nicole. I will be bringing your guests tomorrow night."

"Good night, Claude, and good luck."

As soon as Claude left, I poured the water in the bath and had to add cold water since the buckets had been well heated. I lowered myself into the warm luxury of the bath and scrubbed the filth from my body. I got out and dried myself and put on pyjamas. I dropped my dirty clothes into the bath, adding the remainder of the hot water. I then made myself an omelette, which tasted divine after our near starvation diet of the last few days.

I went into the yard and into the cellar to start making it more comfortable. I brought down the mattress from my spare room and as many blankets and sheets as I could spare. I found pillows, cushions, cups, plates, a tin opener, and some preserved fruit that Eva had given me, so I added some of those as a treat. I was unable to fit chairs through the narrow trapdoor, but I had a collapsible seat, which was virtually flat when closed, and this went through the narrow gap without too much effort. The seat was similar to a school beam with collapsible legs at each end.

The opening was no larger than a narrow skylight without windows and about twelve inches deep and three feet wide. It contained no glass, just old wood from fruit boxes nailed to it. This was draughty but did let a little fresh air in. It was also cold, so I put as many old woollies that I could spare in with the other items. Putting the mattress through was the most difficult part even though it was made of feathers. My constant fear was that Blanche would come into her yard and, although she could not actually see the skylight, hear unusual noises.

Following all this exertion, I drank a glass of milk, fell into bed, and slept late the following morning.

Chapter 12

Sigmund continued to lead his men with brilliant strategies and the unstinted bravery of both himself and his men. Although the Nazis had successes in the Ukraine, the German offensive stalled on the outside of Moscow and was pushed back by a counteroffensive without having taken the city. Following this, the Red Army repelled the Wehrmacht's strongest blow and forced an unprepared Germany into a war of attrition.

Sigmund and his peers learned of this and wondered if some of their men would be sent to fight on another front. During a conversation with another high-ranking officer, the issue of whether or not Hitler was sane enough to make the right decisions was mentioned, and Sigmund's spirits were lifted slightly, knowing he was not the only one questioning Hitler's actions. Sigmund told them of his experiences at Auschwitz and the diabolical atrocities that were carried out by Nazi guards. He also told them that in September they were going to start exterminating Jews at Auschwitz, men women, and children. No comments were made and Sigmund thought he had probably said enough, but he hoped that some of them might ask more questions. It was rumoured that another attempt had been made on Hitler's life but, once again, resulted in failure and the execution of three serving officers.

Sigmund often wondered what Nicole was doing and if she was carrying out rescue operations and keeping Jews from certain extermination. When he thought of her, he felt a pain in his heart. How unbelievable that a German officer should fall desperately in love with a French girl, who he was sure was a resistance member.

His thoughts were brought suddenly to an end when another bombardment started. Everyone knew their duties and efficiently carried them out to the letter. Casualties were dealt with, but medical supplies were running low, although Sigmund had repeatedly requested more, and his wounded troops were suffering unnecessarily. Their orders were to hold their position at all cost as the Ukrainian front was one of the strongest and most successfully defended even though casualties were high.

Sigmund did all in his power to help his troops and tried to comfort the severely injured as much as he could. Many of them were just in their late teens and obviously frightened, even if they tried to hide their fear. Although Sigmund had not received any orders yet, news was coming in that all was not well and that he should expect to be moved to another strategic position. He completely ignored his orders that all Soviet prisoners taken should be starved to death as part of Hitler's "Hunger Plan" and treated his prisoners as well as anyone could treat a prisoner of war. Certainly they were fed and treated as respectfully as possible.

Sigmund was aware that there were various groups that were strongly anti-Hitler, but he didn't know how to get in touch with any and could only pray that some news regarding these factions would come his way. He was sure Nicole would know how to get such information, and he felt quite useless. Nevertheless, he still had to go about his duties and protect his troops, which he did satisfactorily, but he had no stomach for killing and maiming. Nicole had showed him it was possible to have true love for an enemy, and he must remember this when dealing with prisoners.

Chapter 13

Two months passed, and Nicole had little to do other than passing messages to people unknown to her, and to see completely new places, all in the vicinity of the Chateau, and it was both exciting and frightening. Nicole became accustomed to having the family in her cellar and wondered how they kept so quiet which must be a great strain on them all but Nicole knew that if it was her own life was at stake, anything would be possible to preserve it. Occasionally Nicole left milk, water, bread, cheese, and dried meats just outside the narrow trapdoor, but never caught a glimpse of her guests. Of course human waste had to be disposed of each day, and I had to be careful not to let Blanche or somebody who was visiting Blanche see my frequent trips to the privy.

Two days later, Tuesday, 22 August 1941, Major Muller summoned me to the Chateau, actually more like marched me there, escorted by two young SS officers. They were distinctly cold and had the look of true Arians. When I got to the Chateau, I was taken straight to Muller's office. He was strictly polite and asked if I would translate some papers that I suspected had been confiscated from a prisoner or resistant worker. I said I would try but that my English was not good. He passed a file across his desk and gestured for me to take a seat at a little desk on the other side of the room. The transcript was fairly short and bloodstained. I bent over the file, which was obviously to be radioed to England. It told of a small town that had helped several allied troops and Jews escape and because of this, fifty men, women, and children were locked in a church and burnt alive. I found it hard not to cry as my stomach churned from my extreme hatred of the Nazis and their cruelty.

"Where did you get this paper?" I asked Muller, knowing full well that I would not be afforded an answer. "It is very hard to translate as it is not written by an Englishman. I think it was written by a German who knew a little English," I lied. "Knowing German as fluently as I do and knowing only a little English makes translating it confusing. I think it is reporting on an atrocity carried out on a small town but does not say why such a terrible thing was done."

"The content of the letter has nothing to do with you. You are to keep your mouth shut or things can become very difficult for you, even though you are helping us and are a traitor to your own country," said Muller. "I shall be calling on you for further translations, so you are to remain in Blois."

"Do you require me for anything else?" I asked.

"No," was his curt reply.

I decided to see Eva whilst I was there, mainly to see if she had any goodies I could filch. I found her in a very sad mood, mourning her brother who had been killed by a bombing raid over Hamburg.

"I am so sorry, Eva," I said falsely, hoping that I appeared more sincere than I was.

"He was my only brother and was home on leave. It is ironic that you come home safely from fierce fighting only to be killed in your own home," Eva said tearfully.

Not much chance of goodies here, I thought selfishly. However, I was wrong. As I was leaving, she gave me a package containing a large piece of apple strudel and some smoked Bavarian ham.

"Thank you, Eva. It is really kind of you, especially when you have had such bad news." I actually felt a slight pang of guilt—not much though.

I said my good-byes and went off to the bakers where I had to leave a message about the burning of those poor people.

"They must have caught one of our members. The message was on a small piece of bloodstained paper as if it was about to be transmitted. I could not find out anything else—I'm sorry."

"Nicole, you help so much, and we would be in a sorry state if we did not have you," said the baker. He passed me a small loaf of bread. "If all is well, the family will be moved out tonight. I think Claude will be carrying out the evacuation but may need your help."

"That's fine. That poor family has been shut up in that pokey cellar for over two months. They have been as quiet as mice, bless them," I said, hoping that Claude would need my help; it was time my adrenaline started flowing again.

Claude arrived around 1:00 a.m. the following morning. I was dressed and ready to help in any way I could. It was difficult for the adults to get out through the narrow opening in the trapdoor but not so for the children. They were all pale and looked absolutely petrified. Claude put his finger to his lips, although they were quite aware that they had to be completely silent. We made our way to the railway bank and slid down and across the railway into the woods. Claude led the way on a new path that would ultimately lead to a fairly main road. When we got there, we bent low in the undergrowth and then heard a German truck. It stopped where we were hiding, and Claude dragged the children out of the undergrowth and into the back of the truck with the adults following. I was surprised to see that the baker was driving the truck, but I did not recognise the other occupant in the cab. The truck drove off as soon as the family had boarded.

"Where are they going?" I asked Claude.

"Hopefully near La Maison Neuf, where they will be picked up by another truck and, along with a few others, taken to a farm that has a complex underground where they can hide in a bit more comfort and safety."

"Can you find your own way back, Nicole? I have other things to do."

"I am sure I can, Claude. Luckily, there are so few troops about it should not be too dodgy."

We parted with an embrace and went our separate ways. I had a completely uneventful journey home and was soon climbing up the railway bank. As I reached the top, I heard Blanche's shrill voice.

"What on Earth are you doing, Nicole?"

"I saw some torchlight on the other side of the railway line and wondered who it was. Unfortunately, by the time I got down there I could not find anyone. I wondered if someone needed help."

"That was a completely stupid thing to do. You could get us all arrested again," said Blanche angrily. "I know you are up to something and if I find out what it is, I will report you without any hesitation at all."

Blanche then turned and waddled into her house and I thought, *another one I need to be rid of!*

I did not leave the house the following day but did so the next, 25 August, and went first to the Chateau to see Eva and then to the baker's. I informed him that Blanche had caught me getting home and of her threats. I now could only leave it to the rest of them to decide what to do with her, if anything.

Chapter 14

On Saturday, 26 August, Sigmund and his troops received orders to move their location nearer to Leningrad. Hitler had sent an order that Leningrad should be captured first, then Donetsk, and finally Moscow. The Soviet troops were ordered to occupy the territories to the south of Leningrad and the Finnish troops to the north.

On 27 June 1941, the Council of Deputies of the Leningrad administration had organised civilian first-response groups. The whole world had been informed of the danger from the Nazis and over a million citizens were mobilised to fortify Leningrad. Several lines of defences were built along the perimeter of Leningrad in order to repulse hostile forces approaching from north and south by civilian resistance.

Sigmund knew this was going to be a bloody and cruel battle, more of a siege really. Once the Nazis and Finns had achieved their goal of encircling Leningrad and maintaining a blockage, they would prevent all those encircled from receiving food and other supplies. His scientists had advised Hitler that the city would reach starvation after a few weeks.

Sigmund could not believe that such a dreadful plan had been hatched. This was not warfare; it was extermination of all those nationalities that Hitler wished to be rid of. Hitler wanted to exterminate Soviets, but also—as Sigmund had been informed—the plan included exterminating horrendous numbers of Jews at Auschwitz beginning in September by gassing, starvation, and shooting. The train loads of human beings were beginning to arrive at Auschwitz in cattle trucks packed to the gunnels with these poor people in the most degrading circumstances. Newborn babies, he was told, were killed by bashing their tiny heads against anything hard.

Sigmund wracked his brain trying to think of how he could get in touch with someone who, like him, wanted to assassinate Hitler and his equally cruel henchmen. He dared to write a letter to Nicole explaining the events happening—an action of treason that would result in execution for the perpetrator, but he did not care if the letter was intercepted. People should know what was happening to the Jews and Soviets, and Sigmund desperately hoped that the letter would get through.

Sigmund's battalion left the Ukraine for the blockade on Friday, 31 August, and when they arrived on Sunday, 2 September, they found that many prisoners had already been taken, mostly civilians who were doing their best to protect their city with the crudest of weapons. The poor souls did not stand a chance against the heavily equipped Nazis. Some of the largest battles and deadliest atrocities had been carried out to gain the ground surrounding Leningrad that Sigmund and his troops were now there to protect.

Sigmund became acquainted with another high-ranking officer, SS Officer Brundt. They spent many hours talking about the atrocities they were witnessing at the blockade, and Sigmund told him about the plan for the mass extermination of Jews.

"If only someone could do something about Hitler. He must be a madman with several other sadists or madmen at his side," said Brundt.

"I know several attempts on his life were unsuccessful," Sigmund answered.

Sigmund talked to his troops and told them to be as humane as possible when dealing with their prisoners, even sharing food with them. Some of the young soldiers laughed out loud at this, but Sigmund said, "Treat them as you would wish to be treated if you were captured." Of course, the Soviets were as cruel to the Nazis as the Nazis were to them, but even if Sigmund was aware of this, he stood by his orders to his men.

Fighting was fierce with many casualties on both sides, but the Nazis were better equipped than the Soviets. However, what the Soviets lacked in equipment they made up for in strength of character and sheer guts. Sigmund tried to write a letter of condolence to the families of the soldiers fatally injured, but he found this more and more difficult once he realised the futility of the war. He had in his mind the horrific picture of trainloads of Jews arriving at Auschwitz and being herded like cattle. The weak, most of the women, and all of the children went straight to the gas chambers, while strong boys and men went to work camps or factories within the boundaries of Auschwitz.

It was a lift to his spirits when he was informed that he was to take one month's leave as a reward for his battalion's success. He immediately planned to go to Blois to see Nicole by hook or by crook. He was to be driven back to France by one of his men, so he chose a young soldier no more than twenty years old who appeared to be suffering greatly from witnessing the death and destruction. No one knew exactly where the Soviets were, but they never gave up; if the Nazis won a particular piece of land, it was only because every Soviet soldier had been killed or severely injured.

The journey was dangerous, and it took two days for Sigmund to get to Blois and settled into the Chateau. Eva was delighted to see him and asked if he had seen Nicole.

"Not yet, but as soon as I have a bath and get changed I will. I can't wait."

Eva could see the love in his eyes and thought it was a strange world when an enemy falls for someone on the other side.

Sigmund took no time at all getting ready and left the Chateau with a bottle of wine, courtesy of Eva, or rather the Chateau's cellar.

Chapter 15

On Friday, 6 October 1941, Sigmund virtually ran to Nicole's house. The front door was open as usual. He called, "Nicole," but there was no response. Sigmund sat down to wait, feeling a little concerned that Nicole might have been captured while helping someone. His fears were calmed when he heard the back door open and saw a rather grubby looking, but beautiful Nicole standing there, her mouth open in surprise. They simultaneously fell into each other's arms, kissing fiercely and passionately, their tongues probing each other until their mouths were practically numb from kissing. Then Sigmund held her at arm's length.

"*Liebling*, I have missed you with all my heart every minute of every day whilst I have been away from you."

"I can't believe it is really you," replied Nicole. "I must look an absolute sight covered in mud and muck."

"You look beautiful to me. Have you been helping someone?"

"Yes, I think so. I don't always know the outcome of my missions. I must have a bath."

Sigmund's eyes sparkled. "Let me bathe you, my love. Put the water on to heat, and I will get the bath in."

I did not need to be asked again. I filled the buckets and put them on the range, which was still alight. Sigmund lifted the bath in. Neither of us could wait for the water to heat. We started kissing and Sigmund started to undress me.

"You are a messy pup, aren't you? You look as though you have been rolling in the mud for fun."

"No, not for fun—for necessity," I said seriously.

At last the water was warm enough to put in the bath, together with my lavender bath salts. Sigmund removed my last remaining garments, and I got into the bath. Sigmund picked up my sponge and soaped it. He then lent over and gently began to soap my back and then my breasts while bending to kiss and suck my nipples. He caressed my breasts with his hands. I was breathless.

"Stand up, *Liebling*."

I obeyed immediately. He began to wash, kiss, and enter his tongue into my intimate parts. I was weak with wanting him. I stepped out of the bath and as he dried me, he carried out the same foreplay. He took me upstairs, where we made wonderful, genuine love with both of us climaxing simultaneously more than once.

"Oh Sigmund, it is so good that you are home. Are you staying long?"

"About one month."

"I suppose we should get up, drink the bottle of wine to celebrate, and empty the bath. I think we should get some food from the Chateau, as I am entitled to provisions. The walk will do us good and build up our energy for bedtime."

Sigmund's eyes looked adoringly at me. I did not doubt his love for me, and I knew for sure that I loved him with every sinew of my being.

After we emptied the bath and got dressed, we walked to the Chateau to get provisions and saved the wine for later. When we arrived, Sigmund's replacement asked to see him. I stayed in the kitchen with Eva whilst Sigmund dealt with the business of Nazi war plans with SS-Brigadeführer und Generalmajor der Waffen-SS (Brigadier General) Lundz. All we could hear was the murmur of their voices. After about an hour, they both came into the kitchen and Sigmund introduced me to Lundz.

"Nicole, we have been invited to join Brigadier General Lundz for dinner this evening," Sigmund said. "I hope you have not already made plans."

"No, I haven't, and it would be most pleasant to have dinner here. Thank you for your invitation," I replied. After having a general conversation with Eva and Lundz, we took our leave and made our way home to get ready for dinner.

"Do I wear an evening dress?" I asked Sigmund hopefully. It was so long since I had been able to doll myself up,"

"Yes, and I will wear my dress uniform. You won't be able to keep your hands off me." Sigmund laughed.

We had a leisurely stroll back to my house and enjoyed the beginning of a balmy evening. We did not have much time. We were due at the Chateau at 7:30 p.m. for pre-dinner drinks. I decided that I would get dressed in the spare room and took exceptional care with my hair and makeup before putting on an understated but very expensive figure-hugging black dress—old it might be but still in immaculate condition. When Sigmund called up to tell me to get a move on, I slowly walked down the stairs so that he could get the full impact.

"Oh, my dearest girl, you look magnificent. I want you right now,"

"Well, you will have to wait until we get home. I don't want my outfit or makeup ruined. You look so handsome, and there is something I can do that won't ruin your appearance."

As I said this, I unbuttoned his fly and took him in my mouth, just for a few seconds. Nevertheless, this made him tremble and he tried to kiss me.

"No you don't. Be patient—you can think about our lovemaking all evening, as will I."

"I love you, *Liebling*."

"You too, darling."

The evening was very pleasant and laid back. Lundz obviously found me attractive and directed most of his conversation to me. I looked at Sigmund and could see by his eyes that he was jealous. After a while one of the other officers started playing the piano, very well in fact, and ended with the German national anthem, which I could hardly stomach.

"I think we should make a move, don't you, Nicole?"

"Yes, by the time we walk home, it will be nearly midnight."

"Wouldn't you like a car to take you?" enquired Lundz. "I am not sure if it is safe for you to be out alone."

"No thank you. We will be okay," said Sigmund.

We got home safely, and as soon as we shut the front door, Sigmund grabbed me from behind, cupping my breasts in his hands and nuzzling my neck.

"Give me a chance to get my dress off," I said happily. I was about to go upstairs to take off my dress but heard a familiar noise.

"Sigmund, I think I have to go out—someone needs me." I removed my dress and got into warm clothing.

"Nicole, be careful my love."

"I will, don't worry. I have your lovemaking to come home to."

I went silently out the back door and slid down the bank where the baker was waiting.

"Claude has been captured, and I need you to send radio messages to other cells. Someone has given him away we think."

"Do you think it could be my neighbour, Blanche? She may have seen him coming and going with the Jews."

"No. We are pretty sure it is someone in captivity, probably being tortured," whispered the baker.

"What about Sigmund, Nicole? Are you certain he won't give you away?"

"I am putting my life completely and utterly in his hands, and I haven't a single qualm about him giving me away. He really loves me, and I love him. He wants to do something to help. He told me he has seen hell and wants to do his best for all those who are being captured and exterminated by the Nazis. He just does not know how to go about it."

I have never asked the baker's name, because if I don't know it, I can't give him away if I am tortured. We set off wriggling along the ground like reptiles, knowing the German patrols were about in several places; unfortunately, we did not know where. When we got deep into the woodland, it became difficult to move over the wet and soggy ground. Eventually we got to the old piece of flint wall where the radio was situated and I sent all the messages, very risky as the longer you are transmitting the more likely your message will be intercepted. The baker stowed the radio and we set off on a different route. After about half an hour we heard German voices and we stood still hoping that the soldiers would go the other way and not stumble across us. After a while it became apparent the soldiers were there for the night.

In the morning some of the soldiers stayed in their camp whilst the others went off, obviously looking for members of the resistance that had been compromised by those being tortured. I knew that Claude would die before he gave anyone away. We spent the rest of the night and some of the morning laying completely still, which was very hard because our damp clothes were attracting mosquitos and our limbs were aching from lack of movement and cold.

At midday, all the soldiers set out on patrols. Luckily, they did not trip over us but came close enough for us to touch them. We let ten minutes pass and then started wriggling through the brush. After a while we split up, thinking it was easier to hide alone than hide together. My progress was slow going due to stiff joints and the fact that it was daylight. I had to make sure that I was hidden under cover wherever available. Eventually, however, I crawled into my yard. I made sure Blanche was nowhere to be seen and that she could not see me from her windows.

Chapter 16

Sigmund was beside himself when I literally fell into the kitchen on the morning of 8 October, exhausted, wet, and stiff. He picked me up and smothered me with kisses, even though I stank of swampy ground and the perspiration that comes from extreme fear.

"*Liebling*, I thought the worst. The soldiers have been patrolling more or less since you left the house. There is definitely something going on. I brought the bath in and the water is on the range and hot, ready for your bath."

"Thank you, my love. I really can't wait to get into something warm and soothing. I am aching from head to toe," I said, yawning.

Sigmund helped me undress with no sexual thoughts and helped me into the bath. Once I was clean and warm, I got into my pyjamas and went to bed. As Sigmund tucked me in with a loving kiss, I asked, "Do you think you can find out what happened to Claude. He has been captured—given up by a member of the resistance who was being held and tortured. I can't even imagine the atrocities that will be dealt him."

"I will find out as much as I can. Will Claude give you away?"

"Definitely not. I am absolutely sure he would never *grass* on any of us whatever he has to suffer," I said, snuggling down in the bed before dropping into a deep sleep.

When I awoke Sigmund was sitting on the chair in the corner of the bedroom.

"Have you been there all the time I was asleep?"

"Nearly all the time, except for having a coffee. Once you are fully awake and dressed, we will take a walk to the Chateau, and I will try to find out about Claude and any other of your friends that may be in custody." He bent and kissed me gently and lovingly.

About two hours later, we started for the Chateau. Although the air was pleasant for autumn, we still needed to wear warm jerseys. On the way, we passed the baker, but neither of us gave any sign of recognition that we knew each other. When we arrived at the Chateau, we noticed a lot of activity. Lundz came over to Sigmund and started speaking to him quietly. They then went into the office. When they emerged, Sigmund said that I should go home and that he would get back as soon as he could. I knew that something was terribly amiss and walked home very troubled, with a feeling of dread as to what Sigmund would be telling me on his return.

Sigmund arrived home about 7:00 p.m.

"What is it?" I asked anxiously.

"I am so sorry, my darling. Claude and the other prisoners have been executed."

"How? Did you find out who gave them away?" I asked tearfully.

"The prisoners were shot, so at least it was quick. It was one of your own, a young man who was tortured horrendously. No one would have held out against the excruciating pain he had to suffer. Apparently he held out for an unbelievably long time. The other thing, my darling, is that I have been called back to Auschwitz to oversee the work camps and factories where the lucky ones, if you can call them that, work. As long as they stay healthy, they will be kept alive. Lundz said that when the cattle trucks arrive, they are filled to capacity with men, women, and children. I can still see the haunted faces of the little ones from when I was stationed there, and the gassing had not even started." The pain on Sigmund's face left me in no doubt that his sorrow for these poor people was sincere.

"The battles on the Eastern Front are not going according to plan, but Hitler is relentless in his desire to rid the world of the Soviets no matter how many men we lose. Apparently the supplies are not getting through and the troops are hungry. I don't know what will happen when the snow comes and it is below freezing. The German troops only have light clothing and boots," explained Sigmund, who was obviously not in agreement with Adolf Hitler.

"I was wondering if we could go away for a few days, somewhere warm, where we can try and forget the mayhem going on in the world. We could make out we are married." I smiled seductively at Sigmund.

"That would be wonderful, my darling. I could find out the best place to go from Lundz. Maybe Nice would be a good idea, but it depends on the amount of action in the area. I would like you to talk to me in German though, I don't want you to be thought of as a traitor to France," Sigmund said sincerely. "I will go to see Lundz first thing tomorrow. I am sure that I will be allowed a car as long as I agree to go to an area that is safe for German officers and their wives."

Sigmund smiled, apparently thinking lecherous thoughts. We went up to bed and, as usual, made exquisite love. We were unbelievably compatible in all ways. As promised, Sigmund went to the Chateau the following morning and arrived back home with a car and a driver.

"Get packed, we're off. Sorry about the driver, but I am expected to have one. I apologize that our destination isn't Nice, but apparently there is a lovely Chateau near the coast not far from Nice where high-ranking officers like me go for recuperation from the stresses and strains of battle," said Sigmund tongue-in-cheek.

I dashed up the stairs, pulled a suitcase from under my bed, literally threw in some clothes and swimsuits, and shut the lid.

Sigmund laughed. "I see I will have to give you lessons on how to pack, young lady." His case looked immaculate, probably packed by his batman. The cases were stowed in the boot, and we set off on our four-day adventure. I started speaking in German as soon as we were in the car, and the driver looked quite taken aback.

The four days were everything we could wish for: sunbathing, swimming, long, lazy walks, scrumptious food and, as much as I hate to admit it, good company. Best of all, of course, was our uninhibited lovemaking whenever and wherever we had privacy.

On 13 October, we were making our way back to Blois when we came across a broken down truck full of Jews, all wearing yellow stars on their clothes. Most of them were young families, and they looked terrified and in need of sustenance. Sigmund and his driver went to see what had happened. Two of the prisoners were changing a wheel and being shouted at, kicked, and prodded by the guards. Suddenly, several of the captives jumped from the truck and started running for their lives.

More prisoners started to try to escape and in the melee I managed to grab a little boy, about seven years old, who appeared to be alone. I told him in French not to be frightened and bundled him into the boot of the car, stressing he must be very quiet and promising that he would be safe.

The guards continued shouting and firing, shooting at least eight Jews, whether fatally or not I did not know. There were two guards and Sigmund went to talk to them to get the gen on the current situation in the area. No sooner had I done this than the guards came back towards the truck, shoving those who had stopped running back into the truck with a cruel bash from the butt of their guns for good measure. Once they had rounded up of the prisoners, a guard and the driver covered them with their weapons. One of them went to those who had been shot to check to see if they were dead. If not, he made sure that they were before returning to the truck. Sigmund came back to the car and asked if I was all right and said how sorry he was that I had to witness such an incident.

"Actually, Sigmund, I managed to help a little." I looked at Sigmund pleadingly, hoping that he understood what I had done. He did.

When we got going again, he asked me where. As I pretended to kiss his cheek, I whispered, "In the boot. A little boy."

It must have been uncomfortable for the child, and I was trying to think of a way to get him out of the car and into my house without anybody seeing him.

Sigmund said to the driver, "I would like to take the car home this evening, so I will drop you off at the Chateau and bring the car to the Chateau tomorrow morning. I have a surprise for, Nicole."

"Yes, Sir."

Chapter 17

As arranged, the driver was dropped at the Chateau, and Sigmund drove the car to my home. It was dark when we got there and after getting some blankets from indoors, I wrapped the child in a blanket from head to toe and carried him inside. As I lifted him from the boot of the car, Sigmund stood behind me, protecting me from possible prying eyes. First, I had to soothe the child who had no idea what was going on. I asked him where his parents were, but he shook his head and looked sad and forlorn.

I put my arms around his skinny little body and said, "What would you like to eat? Oh I am sorry, I should have asked your name first."

"My name is David Isaacs. I would like some bread, please."

"Well, David, you are safe now. I will look after you until we can get you to a permanent place of safety. I am going to make you some eggy bread and give you a nice fresh glass of milk. You can even have some fruit if you like."

All three of us sat down to "eggy bread" and little David certainly enjoyed it. It had probably been a long time since he had eaten.

"Would you like a bath whilst I make up your bed?" I asked, thankful that I had taken the mattress out of the cellar so it would not get damp.

Sigmund joined us and said in stilted French, 'I will put the water on to heat and bring the bath in. We will have to wash the clothes you have on and dry them in front of the range. I will get you new ones as soon as I can."

David was understandably quiet and wary but had a bath and more milk before we took him upstairs to bed. We all laughed about the blouse and knickers I had given him to sleep in.

"Do you want the light left on, David?" asked Sigmund.

"Yes please, Sir," he replied.

Sigmund immediately told him to call him Sigmund not sir. When we left the bedroom, we told David that we would be downstairs if he wanted anything or was frightened. We sat downstairs having a coffee and waited for David to fall asleep.

"I feel so good and alive," Sigmund said. "I have to find a way to help even a few prisoners escape when I get back to Auschwitz. Is this how you feel when you go on your missions?"

"Yes. It gives me a purpose in life and, although I am usually frightened, I cannot stop trying to help these poor souls and will continue until I am caught or killed," I told Sigmund, leaving him in no doubt that I planned to continue.

The next day, 14 October, Sigmund took the car back to the Chateau and then went round the town buying clothes for his nephew in Germany. He was able to get everything but had forgotten to get the correct size shoes. He would be able to remedy this later in the day after he had delivered his packages to me and David. When I got back, I told him that having found out the size of the shoes I would try and get shoes for him.

The baker was the only person I thought could help with David or, at least, steer me in the right direction. Both Sigmund and I thought they must be careful not to let David see Sigmund in his uniform. Not only would it disturb him, but it would also be dangerous for both myself and Sigmund. I walked passed the bakery and on to a little store where they might have some boys shoes. Fortunately, they had a pair of second-hand shoes in the right size and in fairly good condition. On the way back, I walked passed the bakery again and went in.

"Can I help you?" asked the baker.

"A small loaf please and a potato pie."

"Is there anything else I can help you with?"

"Actually there is. I have a very precious package that I need to send somewhere permanent and safe. I have never dealt with anything like this before."

"You can speak plainly. There is no one here," said the baker.

I related the whole story to him, and he said that I would have to take the child further north so that an aerial pickup could be expedited. I would have to make my own way on public transport closer to the northwest coast where the RAF would make an attempt to pick up David and me, if at all possible. I would have to get to the local church in Brest and would be contacted on my arrival with more detailed arrangements. The baker told me that I would be completely on my own until I got to Brest. All I had to do was work out my journey, get papers for David, and notify the baker when I would be arriving in Brest.

When I got home, Sigmund and David were chatting quite amiably in French, although Sigmund was struggling a bit, which made David laugh. It was so good to see that this little boy could still laugh. Once he had a few solid meals inside him, he would be stronger and fit to travel. David liked his shoes and the rest of his outfits and was really pleased that he had pyjamas!

When David was in bed, I discussed arrangements with Sigmund. I asked him to get me papers for David in my name, de Bois. I explained to him that I had to take David to Brest where the RAF would pick him up and that I would probably go with him. He will pass as my nephew and act as if we were going on a trip to Brest to see his uncle, a priest in that town.

"It is going to be difficult to get papers for him. It may be necessary for you to get counterfeit ones that I can sign and stamp with official Nazi stamps," Sigmund said worriedly. "It is going to be very dangerous for you, Nicole, and how will I know when you are back in France?"

"I don't know how we will get in contact, but we will manage somehow. I may be able to come to Poland to help you save a few dear souls," I said, feeling excitement at the thought of helping Sigmund free some prisoners from the death camps at Auschwitz.

The next day I told David that his surname was de Bois and that he must be certain to always remember that. I explained that he was my nephew, and we would be going on trip to see his uncle who was a priest in Brest.

"You must never, never let anyone know you are Jewish, David. Otherwise, you and I will probably be killed," I said this forcibly. He was young and had seen such terrible things, but I had to be straight with him in order to keep us safe.

By Friday, 20 October, Sigmund had stamped and signed papers for David, papers purloined somehow by the baker. Sigmund had also gotten us tickets to Brest via a route with several changes of buses and trains, and we should arrive in Brest two days later on Tuesday, 24 October, God willing. Sigmund would also be leaving on Saturday, 21 October, to go to Auschwitz. Our last night together was filled with passionate lovemaking, a pledge of undying love for each other, and sadness because we would be parted for a considerable time.

"Marry me, Nicole. Please, please, my darling, marry me."

"If I manage to get David safely delivered to a family in England, I will try to get to you in Auschwitz and then we can get married. We can try to help prisoners escape as we discussed."

We kissed passionately again, touching each other in the erotic places that had become familiar to us and then bringing each other to an ultimate exquisite climax.

The following morning we were filled with sadness at our separation. Sigmund was the first to leave. His driver picked him up at eight. It was difficult to explain to David why Sigmund was dressed in the uniform of a high-ranking SS officer, but we told him that it was to enable me to get him to safety.

Chapter 18

We left at 10:00 a.m. and walked slowly to the railway station where we hoped to get a train that would be going in the direction of St. Malo. We should be able to alight at Nantes where we hoped to get a bus or even a lift on the Nantes to Brest canal. Our wait was long at the station, and David was restless and difficult to placate. There were several German troopers on the platform, and I did not want unnecessary attention. So I spoke sternly to David, telling him that we were in danger and he must behave normally.

Eventually a train arrived at midday. It was fairly empty, which was a bonus, and we managed to get a two-seater space at the back of one of the carriages, away from any attention. The train was slow, and each stop filled me with fear as more troopers got on. David had settled down and was reading a book. It was a tremendous relief when we arrived at Nantes. My heart was in my mouth when I handed our tickets to the ticket collector, but all went smoothly. We were on the streets of Nantes in late afternoon when David said he was hungry, as was I, so we went into a little café that appeared empty. The proprietor said that there was soup or an omelette on the menu, and I said we would like both if possible.

"Yes, we have been quiet and have plenty eggs and vegetable soup. Do you want bread?"

"Yes please, that would be lovely. Have you any milk for my nephew? I would like a coffee please," I said pleasantly.

"There is some lovely fresh milk from our own cows, which I am sure your nephew would like. Where are you from? I have not seen you around this area before."

"We are from Blois and are on our way to see my nephew's uncle, who is a priest in Brest."

The proprietor made no further comment. He began heating the soup and making the omelettes, and he poured milk for David and coffee for me.

"Thank you, Sir" said David politely. When he received the milk, he drank it thirstily.

"That was really nice," David said with a smile, perhaps hoping he might be offered more, but none was forthcoming. The soup and omelettes were good and the bread fresh.

"Do you know if there is a bus that will take us to Brest?" I asked.

"There is, but I think it goes in the morning."

I settled the bill and we left the café. I decided to go to the bus station and find out about the bus to Brest. The café owner had been right: the bus would leave at eleven the following morning. As we were leaving the bus station, two German soldiers approached us.

"What are you doing here?" asked the bespectacled soldier.

"We are trying to get a bus to Brest where we are meeting my nephew's maternal uncle, who is a priest in Brest," I said calmly.

"Can we see your passes and identifications?" asked the other soldier.

It was more an order than a request. When I handed over the papers, they both took note of who had signed them and their attitudes changed slightly.

"You will have to find somewhere to stay tonight during the curfew. There is a hotel of sorts in the next road that may be suitable. In any event, you must stay somewhere during the curfew."

"Thank you. We will go there and see if they have a vacancy," I replied.

The soldiers left the bus station, and we followed. We walked down the next road and found the hotel. A pleasant, rather large woman came to the reception and informed me that she had a twin-bedded room.

"By the way, my name is Elizabeth. I can offer you an evening meal, not much but filling and nourishing. The produce is from our smallholding. The Germans leave us enough to feed ourselves, good of them, don't you think?" she said sarcastically.

"That would be extremely kind of you, Elizabeth. My name is Nicole, and this is my nephew David. We are from Blois and are going by bus tomorrow to Brest to visit David's maternal uncle, who is a priest there." Elizabeth took us to our bedroom, and I decided there and then that we both would be sleeping on top of the covers with our clothes on!

We spent an extremely pleasant evening with a nourishing meal, red wine for me and milk for David, and a constant diatribe from Elizabeth. We went to bed at ten and slept reasonably well. Elizabeth had some fresh bread and coffee for our breakfast and, after settling up with her, we took our leave and went to the bus station. We had an extremely uneventful journey, although there were many German soldiers about, and arrived at Brest safe and sound on Tuesday, 24 October 1941. I enquired about the church from a local passerby and eventually got there. As we entered, the priest came towards us, picked David up, kissed his cheeks, and then put him down; he kissed me too.

"Hello, Nicole, lovely to see you again. It is especially lovely to see you, David. My how you have grown." David looked bewildered but said nothing. I was amazed at how efficient the underground movement had been.

"Do you know when the package will be picked up?" I asked.

"If all goes well, tonight. There is apparently no moon because of the mist and low cloud cover, but of course it is dangerous for the pilot."

The rest of the afternoon and evening dragged interminably, but at last the priest came to where we were sitting and said it was time to go.

"Don't forget it is curfew. We must remain hidden at all times. There are frequent patrols, but I think we have worked out their pattern. It is about one mile to the field. From now on no speaking," he stressed.

Apart from one hurried entry into someone's house, to let the patrol go by, we arrived at the designated field. There were several men and women there, and when we heard the engine of a light plane they all lit candles. The plane landed safely, and David and I were unceremoniously dumped inside without the plane actually coming to a halt.

We were soon in the air and the pilot said, "Keep your eyes out for the Luftwaffe although I am not expecting trouble. We have some company with us, but two sets of eyes are better than one."

They never ceased to impress me with their bravery and jollity. After a very bumpy and tense flight, we landed at Biggin Hill Airport where a senior officer and a social worker met us. After I gave him the briefest cuddle and kiss, David was whisked away.

"God bless, David. I hope you will be very happy," I said.

The senior officer took me into a boardroom of sorts where I related the happenings of my time in France. They were extremely interested in the roundup of Jews and other minorities and that the factory at Auschwitz was producing synthetic rubber. I told them as much as I knew about the Eastern Front and the vast numbers of German troops deployed in Operation Barbarossa. General Kitts, the most senior officer there, shook my hand.

"You have done a wonderful, brave, and sterling job, Nicole, well beyond the remit that anyone could ask for. The information that you have transmitted in dangerous circumstances has saved many lives. Thank you from all those concerned. I expect you would like see your overnight accommodation and freshen up, and then we can all meet in the mess for a meal and, of course, a celebratory drink to your safe return."

After a shower, I changed into the only other outfit I had with me and went to the mess. The meal was surprisingly good and afterward, we had a good old "drink up," similar to those I had when at university. I actually staggered to bed and woke the following morning with one hell of a hangover. I was forced to eat a cooked breakfast and drink copious amounts of coffee and felt slightly better. I thought of the old adage, *never again*. General Kitts asked to see me, so I went to his office.

"Come in, Nicole. I hope you enjoyed our little bash last night."

"Yes, Sir, I certainly did, but I am paying for the excesses today," I replied.

"I was wondering what you are going to do now."

"Well, the first thing is to see my parents. I have had no contact with them whilst I have been in France. I will then have a short rest to regain my fitness. I have met and fallen in love with a senior SS officer, Sigmund Lubisch, and I promised him that I would go to Auschwitz where he is posted to help him with the escape of as many Jews as possible.

"He has helped me in the past with my missions and is quite distraught at the barbaric cruelty of Hitler in his treatment of Jews and other minorities. As I think I mentioned last night, he told me that the treatment of the Russian soldiers on the Eastern Front was unbelievable—that they were left to starve to death. I have no idea how I am going to get to Poland. I will have to go from France where my house is so as not to cause suspicion. Sigmund has been trying to find like minds that can actually make an attempt on Hitler's life, but it is risky without knowing whom to trust. I was wondering if you could get me back to France after I have seen my parents, so I can get in touch with the resistance fighters who might have contact with the resistance in Poland. Most of the Jews from France have been sent there."

"I will see what can be done. We always have need of a courier to go to France on various matters and this could be your way back. It is a jolly risky thing you are undertaking.

How are you going to explain your contacting this German fellow?" he asked.

"I am going to marry him, Sir."

General Kitts looked dumbfounded and did not know what to say other than to wish me good luck. "I suppose I don't have to tell you how risky this sort of relationship can be. If you fall out, he may betray you."

"Never, He genuinely loves me and hates Hitler for the dreadful atrocities carried out and wants to help as many people escape as possible. Obviously, we have no pie-in-the-sky ideas that we can help hundreds, but if we help just a few, it would be of great importance to both of us."

"I must not detain you anymore. Get in touch with only me when you want to go back, Nicole. Have you any idea how long it might be?"

"Not exactly. I would like to have at least a couple of weeks with my parents. I will not be telling them of my plans, not the true ones in any event."

I left General Kitts's office and picked up my case. A car had been sent to take me to my parents' home in Sandwich, Kent. I was really excited about seeing them and surprising them with my visit. It was 26 October 1941, only five days after kissing my lover good-bye. I thought about Sigmund constantly and prayed that he would be safe and mentally able to cope with the horrors that he would undoubtedly come across.

Chapter 19

I asked the driver to drop me at the beginning of the lane where my parents lived in a small, cosy bungalow so that I could surprise them. I went round the back and let myself in through the conservatory, somewhat surprised that my parents weren't napping. I went into the sitting room and found them reading the papers.

"Surprise! Surprise!" I shouted probably a little too loud, but the joy on their faces was a sight to behold.

"Nicole, my darling girl! Why didn't you tell us you were coming? I don't have 'anything in' for dinner," said my forever-practical mother whilst my father, as usual, reverted to his native French and welcomed me warmly.

"How are you? Are you keeping well? Can you tell us where you have been?" they asked almost in unison.

"I can't. Everything is all hush hush, but I am very well as you can see. I think I may have lost a few pounds, but military rations are not exactly palatable," I said laughingly. "How are you both? Have you had many raids?"

Father answered in English that they were both fine, and then said, "We have had quite a few raids due to our proximity to the sea but nothing as bad as in other places. I am in the Home Guard, would you believe!" he said proudly.

"I would not expect anything less," I said, beaming at this dear man.

We all gabbled on about this and about friends of mine who had sadly been killed fighting in France, and also about others who were still safe.

Mother then asked the inevitable. "How long are you home for, Nicole?"

"I think about two weeks, so we have plenty of time to share with each other. Is it all right if I have a bath? I have been dreaming of a good soak."

"Peter"—Mother had always called Dad by his English name—"put the emersion on. It won't take long to heat up, Nicole, but we conserve as much energy as we can, just in case."

"Just in case of what?" I laughed. Mother loved to worry. Goodness knows what my father has to put up with when I am away.

After I had had a long soak and put on my pyjamas—something that helped me feel relaxed whilst listening to the radio, reading, or chatting—Mother rustled up a rather nice meal, especially as she had "nothing in!" They reared their own chickens and Father had a flourishing vegetable garden, fruit trees, and soft fruit canes. Mother roasted a chicken, and we had it with the last of the runner beans and carrots. She also made a delicious crumble from what was left on the fruit canes, and we had custard!

The time rushed by and we all turned in around midnight. I found it quite noisy, with aircraft going overhead on bombing missions in Germany. I had forgotten how close we were to several airfields, and I wished the soldiers a safe return. I lay for quite a while thinking of Sigmund, missing him dreadfully, and worrying about him. I loved him with all my heart and longed to be with him.

The next day we walked round the village and met many friends who were full of questions about how I was and how long I was on leave. We had lunch in our local. There was plenty of produce about as most of the residents of Sandwich had turned part or all of their gardens into vegetable gardens and kept chickens and even sheep if their garden was big enough. The meal was lovely, and we washed it down with a pint of real ale made in a microbrewery by a group of elderly gents, who apparently loved brewing it. It was indeed very palatable.

Each day was filled with shopping, visiting, walking, and just enjoying one another. On one of our shopping expeditions, I bought a beautiful outfit for my reunion with Sigmund. I could see the question in Mum's eyes, but I did not enlighten her.

On the evening of Saturday, 11 November, the air raid siren went off. Mother gathered a bag of essentials that she always had ready for such an occurrence, and we made our way to the Anderson shelter. The noise was incredible: the drone of bombers, the whining of RAF planes as they fought their usual brilliant fight, and the occasional huge blast when a bomb landed and shook the ground. We, thankfully, were not affected apart from the fact that as a member of the Home Guard, Father was called out to assist those who had been bombed and to watch for parachuting Germans. The raid continued, on and off, until the all clear sounded at 11:00 a.m. the next day. The nearest airfield had been badly damaged and a row of terraced cottages hit with two fatalities and several injuries. Mother and I went into the house to have a relaxing cup of tea and a late breakfast.

"Will Dad be back soon?" I enquired.

"I don't know. It depends on the damage and the number of injuries, fires, and downed aircraft."

In fact, Dad did not come back until the next day, absolutely shattered, and went off to bed as soon as he had had his breakfast and tea. Later that day I had a call from General Kitts saying that I would be able to go to my required destination on Wednesday 15 November weather permitting. I would have to accompany another agent and be his radio operator until he was *au fait* with the ins and outs of undercover work and fully integrated with a cell. I think General Kitts was actually setting a test for me. I said that would be fine, and he asked me to come to see him to get coordinates face-to-face and meet the other agent. A car would come for me the next morning at ten.

When I walked into General Kitts's office, there was a very handsome young man sitting there. "Good morning. Lovely to see you again. How are you?" General Kitts asked.

"Very well thank you, Sir," I answered.

"This is the agent who is going with you. You will land about five miles from the town of Auschwitz where members of the Polish resistance will be meet you."

Neither the young man nor I were told each other's names, a strict rule which we always adhered to. I would be at a disadvantage this time, as I did not speak Polish. Apparently the other agent did, so he would translate for me if necessary. No doubt, however, the resistance cell would have English-speaking members.

When the car arrived for me on 15 November, I hugged my parents who pleaded with me to be careful even though they had no idea what I actually did. I was dressed in my RAF uniform, which of course was just a guise and would be left behind when we set out on this mission. The sky was very cloudy, but the weather was dry and calm and ideal for the light aircraft that would be taking us to Poland. There was also a light mist but not bad enough to stop our flight.

We took off at 10:00 p.m. with the good wishes of General Kitts and his team. Our pilot told us that when we landed he would not stop completely, and we were to throw out our cases and jump. Once we retrieved our cases, we were to run to the right, almost the same instructions I had been given when I first went to France. Of course, I did not know the other agent on that mission or even his nationality. He went off on his own mission and whether he survived or not, I will never know.

Chapter 20

When we came nearer to our landing site we were fired at. The pilot went to a higher altitude and there was quite a lot of turbulence.

"We might have to try an alternative landing site," said the pilot calmly, "but I would prefer to wait and see for a while. Sorry about the turbulence, but I must keep high until I am sure that we are fairly safe."

We flew, or rather bumped and shook, for half an hour. Finally, the pilot said that he was going in and that we should be ready to vacate the plane as soon as it was moving slowly enough to jump without causing injuries. I was surprised at how nervous I was this time. Not being able to speak or understand Polish made me uncomfortable.

We bounced a bit when we landed and soon the pilot shouted, "Go!"

We both threw out our cases and jumped after them, not easy when you are still bumping along an uneven field. We retrieved our cases and ran in the direction we had been told. There was no one in sight, and we hid as best we could. It was drizzling and cold, but we waited for at least an hour and still no one came.

We were both too frightened to speak, but I whispered, "Do you think we are in the right place?"

"I don't know. Obviously, the pilot had been given an alternative plan, so let's hope someone comes soon."

We were both pretty bruised from jumping out of the plane, and we were cold, wet, and miserable. At last someone came and quietly gestured us to follow him. He was unkempt and looked as if he could do with a good feed. It was already dawn so we had to get to wherever we were going as quickly as possible. This turned out to be a derelict building where there were several men huddled together.

Their spokesman, a middle-aged man, asked in good English, "Have you a radio?"

"Yes," I answered.

"We need to send a message as soon as possible."

I took out my radio, and the spokesman dictated in English what I had to send, which was a summary of the atrocities that were being carried out by the Nazis and the extermination of Jews who were being brought into the death camps by the trainload. It was heartbreaking and sickening. I wondered if Sigmund had been able to save anyone and if he had been successful in finding an ally in trying to get rid of Hitler.

The Polish spokesman said, "We must move. The Nazis may have picked up our signal. Keep in the shadows as much as possible and do not speak. We have about two miles to go, and there are many Nazi patrols around."

We left our position and walked in single file, hiding in the shadows of derelict, bombed buildings, and woodland where possible. Our trek ended in a damp cellar of a virtually non-existent building that appeared ready to collapse. There were several families living in squalor and all looked hungry. We were shown a corner of the room where we could keep our bits and pieces. Selfishly, I worried about keeping my special outfit dry and in good condition for when I met Sigmund. Just thinking about our meeting made me ache for him.

A few more men arrived with bread, salami, eggs, cheese covered in mould, water, and what appeared to be squirrels. One of the women took the mould off the cheese, and the food was distributed fairly. The relief on people's faces was clear. I had some chocolate, which I shared with everyone, and I refused the other food. I had eaten plenty in the past days and weeks, so going without for a day would certainly not be a hardship.

The following day I started to teach the allocated Pole and the agent who came with me how to use the radio. Both of them picked it up incredibly fast, but I stressed that they must not use it again in this location and should go to different places for each message. That evening after curfew, we all went out in groups and in different directions. When we got to our destinations, we found quivering wrecks of human beings, mainly Jews, waiting to be led to comparative safety.

The group I was with was a group of five, three women and two children, and we took them stealthily to a large and grand house, somewhat damaged by shrapnel and with many shattered windows. The owners, Polish nationals, welcomed them warmly, and we left them in their care and then risked getting back to the cellar. The leader of our group knew all the underground tunnels and ruins, and we made it back safely.

Once we were back, we heard gunfire and realized one of our groups had not returned. Whether they were able to deliver their precious cargo, we would never know or whether any resistance members had been killed. In any event, we had to move our position in case someone was caught, tortured, and, confessed while unbearable pain was inflicted on them. So the next evening, travelling in small groups, even just in pairs, we moved to another location.

I had no idea where we were, and the only English-speaking members were in the other groups; probably so that I did not glean too much information as I was still under suspicion. On 18 November, we ended up in what I presumed to be the ruins of a hospital or care home. The pungent smell of urine permeated the only intact rooms. When all the remaining members of the resistance arrived, less those who were missing and presumed captured, I was asked to send another radio message, this time dictated in Polish so each word had to be spelt out. I reiterated that we should move once the radio message was sent, but I was told there was no possibility that we could move. I explained to the resistance members that I had to get to the Auschwitz camp as soon as I could.

"I have taught your two members how to send messages, and they have picked it up extremely well."

"Are you able to tell us the reason for your visit to the camp?" the Pole asked.

"I am not able to divulge any information. I'm sorry," I answered. "I need to know where I can contact you. I will try to get some bits of food for you, and I will need your help in getting some precious cargo out of Poland."

"Well, we can draw you a map of a local church in Auschwitz, but that is the best we can do," the Pole said. "You can leave a message and anything else behind the altar. We will leave messages there for you, too. It is a very safe place, at least for the moment."

"That is fine. Thank you."

This, in fact, was ideal. I could find somewhere to stay where there were plenty of Germans, and I could get ready for my longed for meeting with Sigmund.

Chapter 21

I left the hideout on 19 November and started my journey to the town of Auschwitz. I asked a couple of German soldiers where I could find a place to stay for a few days whilst visiting a friend. They told me of a hotel near the camps where SS officers stayed when their families came to visit.

"Who are you here to see?" asked one soldier.

"Lieutenant Colonel Sigmund Lubisch."

"I think he is off duty today, but you will find him in the officers' accommodation in the barracks. If you ask the sentry, he will put a call through to him, and he will then come to fetch you."

I thanked them for their assistance and made my way to the hotel as directed. The receptionist, a German woman, showed me to a pleasant room overlooking the gardens at the back of the building. I bathed and put on my special underclothes and outfit and admired myself, vainly, in the mirror. I hoped Sigmund would like what he saw.

It was bitterly cold as I walked towards the barracks, aware of the sickly smell of death in the smoke and in the air wafting on the slight breeze. I wondered how the families of the Nazis could bear to come to such a place but, of course, I was doing just that. When I got to the barracks, I went to one of the sentry boxes and asked to see Lieutenant Colonel Lubisch. The sentry looked me up and down admiringly, picked up his phone, checked his list, and dialled a number.

"What is the nature of your visit?" he asked.

"A social call."

"Your name?"

"Nicole du Bois," I answered in perfect German.

After what seemed an age, but was only a matter of a few minutes, Sigmund stood in front of me, a magnificent figure of a man with those fabulous eyes. He smiled broadly, put his arms around me, and kissed me, not as passionately as I would have liked, but after all he was in front of his subordinate.

"Nicole, I can't believe it. I have been waiting impatiently for you to get here. Come, we can go to my mess room to get my coat, and then we can find somewhere for you to stay."

"I have already booked into the hotel. I have been longing to see you."

"Me too, my darling." When we reached his room, we literally flung off our clothes and melted into one. It was heavenly but over far too quickly.

"Never mind, we can have a lovely night together making love from dusk to dawn," Sigmund said huskily. We started to kiss again but stopped before it all went too far again. We dressed and Sigmund sent for a car to take us to the hotel.

We had to be so careful what we said to each other, and to stay safe, I only told him what I had been up to. I asked what his plans were as we walked through a park that I had seen on my way to the barracks. At the hotel, the receptionist recognized Sigmund and was very servile.

"I want the best double room you have, or even a suite if you have one."

"Indeed we do, Sir, the bridal suite," the receptionist said coyly.

"Very appropriate under the circumstances," Sigmund said.

"My clothes and case are in another room, Sigmund."

"That's okay. Arrange for them to be brought to our suite," he told the receptionist.

"Certainly, Sir."

The suite was delightful, though old fashioned, and it would be like our little home.

"Can we go for a walk before dinner, Sigmund?"

"What! I want to ravish you," he laughingly said, "but actually I think that is a good idea." We put on our coats and scarves and set off for the park.

"We must not talk within the earshot of anybody. We don't want to make anyone suspicious, do we? I managed to get David to England safely and handed him over to the authorities and then spent time with my parents. They have no idea what I do, and they think I work in the RAF intelligence department. I have been with the Polish resistance since I came back. These poor people are suffering dreadfully. At least I know the radio call sign for when we rescue some of the Jews, so that I can take them to the resistance for onward passage to the allies. I can't bear to think what is causing that dreadful smell, but of course I know full well what it is. Have you come up with a plan for how we are going to help some to escape?"

"The only possible way is to apprehend a man or a boy coming back from the factory. The women and children are exterminated on arrival at the main camp. I cannot understand how soldiers just herd these poor naked people into the gas chambers and carry on laughing and chatting as though they were in a pub. It is truly horrendous, Nicole. I cannot find anyone who will even hint at getting rid of Hitler. People are looking out for themselves. Another way is to employ some women from the camps when we are married. We can save them in that way, and one or two could possibly even escape."

"Have you any idea when we will be married? I have a false German birth certificate, and the sooner we marry, the sooner we can put our plans into action."

I was so anxious to help someone escape from hell that I was quite brazen and did not give a damn.

"We can marry straight away. I will speak to the camp priest and obtain permission from my senior officer. We can have a house in the town. I am afraid it will have belonged to a Jew more than likely, but we have no choice."

"I will be keeping in touch with the resistance as much as I can and get them food, but I will not tell you when I will be carrying this out so you won't need to worry about it. We will need their assistance once we start getting people out."

"Well, my darling, let's get back to our suite and make long, passionate love," Sigmund said.

We held hands and laughed as we ran back to the hotel, acting as if we did not have a care in the world. We went to dinner wearing broad smiles after having had a "quickie" as an aperitif! After our meal and a few drinks, we went to our suite. Once there we had a leisurely bath together with our usual extreme petting, but once in bed, all we wanted to do was hold each other's naked bodies close whilst whispering words of love.

In the morning Sigmund obviously had to go back to the factory but said he would start arranging our marriage and getting our house.

"A house with a cellar that is as remote as possible would be a good idea," I reminded him.

"Anything you say, *Leibling*. Come and kiss me good-bye before I leave for that hell hole of a camp." We kissed and as usual it became passionate, and I pushed Sigmund away.

"There is no time, my darling, you must be going."

"I hope to get back at a reasonable time this evening. Be careful in whatever you are going to do," Sigmund said, looking concerned.

"Even I cannot kill Hitler on my own," I said laughingly.

Once Sigmund had left I showered, made up, and dressed carefully. I went to the dining room where there were a couple of German women sitting and chatting. I went to them and introduced myself. We chatted amiably but kept clear of mentioning the camps.

"Do you know where I can buy some makeup locally?" I asked.

The two women, Gilda and Sylvia, gave me directions, and I set off to do some shopping. The shopping area was about one mile from the hotel, and because of the large German presence in the vicinity, there was quite a selection of most things. There were shops where only Germans could go, and the first things I bought were makeup, silk stockings, bath salts, and a lovely silk blouse of pure white, embroidered by hand with exquisite skill.

I wandered around the market and bought bits and pieces of food, nothing too much to attract attention. I then walked to the church. I put a scarf over my head and went inside. The church was empty, and I left my little packages of food and coffee behind the altar and left. I walked slowly back to the hotel glad that I was well wrapped up as it was bitterly cold and starting to snow. As I entered the hotel, Gilda and Sylvia came over and asked if I had gotten what I wanted.

"Yes, thanks. I also got a beautiful blouse that will do for my wedding." I showed them the blouse and the beautiful and fine embroidery struck them.

"I will have to find a nice skirt now to go with it."

Sylvia immediately said, "There is a woman who makes many things for us. She is a very talented dressmaker, and I am sure she would be happy to make you a skirt to match your blouse. You could probably get some material in town, but it is not particularly easy to get hold of quality cloth."

"Where does the woman live?" I asked Sylvia.

"In the camp, there are several useful people that are skilled, and this keeps them alive as well," Sylvia said callously. "We often get them to do tasks. When you get your house, you will be able to get superb cleaners, as they vie for the posts in order to survive."

I immediately hated this woman for the contempt she had for the Jews, which I could see on her face and hear in her words.

Chapter 22

I made my farewells and went up to the suite. I was amazed at the quality of the makeup, which was only available to Nazis, but I must act as one of them in order to carry out our missions. I was anxious to get on with our work but knew I must be patient. We had the wedding to plan and would have to spend it amongst these awful people. Surely there must be some like-minded Germans. They can't all be murderous thugs. Of course, I knew there were plenty that were kind and distraught at what the *führer* was ordering to be carried out, but I could not understand how they just went about the absolute slaughter of men, women, and children—even babies. Sigmund was one of those who intended to do what he could, and I believe Eva at the Chateau at Blois was another, if there was some way we could safely assess her genuine thoughts. As soon as we had our house, we could start our work. I just could not wait.

Our marriage was arranged for Friday, 8 December. It was held in the church where I dealt with my friends in the resistance. It was a bitterly cold, wet day and I shivered in my lovely lace blouse, worn with a pencil-slim skirt of navy blue. My hair was shining after a wash with expensive shampoo and a long brushing, and I wore a little diamante clip in it.

When I reached Sigmund's side at the altar, he turned to me and said, "You look beautiful, my darling."

I felt really emotional and could not answer him but could only look at this wonderful specimen of manhood that was going to be my husband in a few minutes. The priest carried out just a short version of the marriage ceremony, and in no time at all we were walking hand in hand out of the church and being showered with confetti by the few who attended the service.

There was a car outside the church and Sigmund said, "I have arranged a short honeymoon in a quiet little village not too faraway. I am sorry that this is just a trivial gift to my most beautiful and deeply loved wife."

"Oh, Sigmund, it is a lovely idea. I feel so proud to have you as my husband, and I can't wait to be in your arms now and forever. I also look forward to our mission."

It was about an hour's drive, and Sigmund drove the car himself. The house was traditional and old, but very picturesque with large gardens.

"Darling, this is our home for the time I am stationed here. It is in a secluded area, and you and I can begin our work as soon as we want."

"Sigmund, I love you with all my heart and thank you for your promise to help me help others."

As I said these words, tears ran down my face and Sigmund kissed them away and held me close. In no time at all we were in our bed, making long, sensuous love until we both exploded in a climax that physically exhausted us. We got up late the following morning, had breakfast, and then went exploring the surrounding countryside. We found many secluded copses, small caves, and ditches where we could hide escapees.

"I have to go to the church to see if there is a message for me," I said to Sigmund.

"I will go with you, it would seem natural for us to visit the church where we made our vows."

After our exploratory walk, we went home, had a snack, and then went back to the church. There was no message for me, but I left a message in code, explaining where I could be found and that we had found places where we could hide those lucky enough to avoid the camps.

When we got back, we actually explored our new home. It was charming and beautifully furnished. I felt rather guilty that this home belonged to a family who may have been exterminated, but this made me even more determined to save as many people as possible, whatever the cost to either myself or Sigmund. We had just settled down on the couch when there was a banging on the door. Sigmund opened the door and without a by-your-leave several SS officers and their wives or girlfriends came in with wine, beer, cheese, and homemade titbits.

"You did not think you were going to get away without our celebrating your marriage," said a large man called Herman.

Everyone was in extremely high spirits and the party went on until the middle of the night, with virtually everyone ending up worse for wear. Gradually everyone said their farewells, making us promise to visit them in their stolen homes. It appeared that they couldn't give two hoots about the previous owners or what happened to them.

After another night of exquisite and satisfying lovemaking, we got up about nine. It was Sunday, 10 December, and we decided to go to church to see if I had a message—after the service of course. We vowed that from this day forward, we would both do our best to help as many people as we could to escape Nazi cruelty. The service was pleasant, but, of course, mainly aimed at the Nazis who made up most of the congregation.

After the service, I asked the priest if I could be responsible for putting whatever flowers I could get hold of in the church. He was more than happy for this to happen, and it would give me a legitimate reason to visit the church often without arousing suspicion. I then went to the back of the altar and retrieved a message. A young Jewish girl was in the hands of the resistance, and I needed to hide her until they were able to get her away from the area. This entailed the resistance making a chain of hideouts until they could get her to the allied occupied areas, which took a lot of planning. They preferred to get as many as they could to safety at the same time. I would meet her at the church the next morning—my first day to arrange flowers!

When Sigmund and I got home, we discussed getting a girl from the camp to come and clean the house. We would be able to feed and nurture her and if Sigmund could arrange to drive her, he would attempt to hide someone else in the boot at the same time. There were so many prisoners aimlessly walking to the factory camp dazed and starving that no one would miss one. If one went missing, the person would be assumed dead. The only real danger was somebody splitting on Sigmund.

We would deal with the Jewish girl tomorrow and see how it goes. I intended to see what flowers or evergreen plants were available and take them to the church before making my way back through the woods and fields to the house with the girl. The only hazard would be if there was someone else in the church, but I was sure the resistance would not leave her there, or even take her there, if that was the case.

Sigmund was back at work the next morning and was already gone when I left for the church. I strolled leisurely through the town and managed to get some flowers and greenery. I had no idea what they were, but they were creamy white and went well with the greenery. When I reached the church there was nobody there. I went to the alcove behind the altar, but it was empty. I busied myself arranging the flowers and, though I say so myself, they looked fine. I heard a noise and looked up. The priest was standing by the vestry door beckoning me to go to him. Once inside the vestry, I saw a young woman, probably about nineteen years old, who looked pale and frightened. The priest, whose name was Novotny, introduced me to the girl named Ruth. I put my arms round her and felt her thin, frail body, which was literally shaking with fear. Luckily, the priest spoke German and translated my words into Polish.

"Nicole is going to look after you until arrangements can be made to get you to the allies and ultimately to England. You must follow her actions, as she does not speak or understand Polish."

Ruth smiled and thanked me in English followed by *dziekuje* in Polish.

I said that I had brought with me a good quality coat for Ruth to wear. She would not look so scruffy and hopefully not suspicious in case we were seen. We set off out from the vestry's back door and walked past a few graves to a short wall. This we climbed and made our way to the woods. Once in the woods, I took Ruth's hand and led her into a narrow gully that probably had water running through it at on time or other but now gave us extra cover. The worst part would be the fields that were empty of most crops except sugar beet, which did not grow more than a foot high. Nevertheless, we made it to the house without a hitch. Ruth looked round and realised that it had belonged to a Jewish family and had been confiscated by the Nazis.

"Do you understand English, Ruth?" I asked.

"Yes, a little," she answered timidly.

"You will have to stay hidden in this house until I hear from the resistance. I don't know for how long, but we will keep you as safe as we can. My husband is a German SS officer."

It was very laborious trying to get Ruth to understand, but I showed her my wedding ring and a picture of Sigmund. When she finally understood, I saw the look of astonishment on her face. I took her to her room on the first floor and showed her the bathroom she would be using. I showed her the clothes that I had for her and some makeup.

"If anybody comes to the house, you must stay in your room in silence," I explained and hoped she understood. I began to realise that her English was fairly good.

I left her to get used to her surroundings and made soup for us to have with some bread. I fetched Ruth down, and we sat at the kitchen table eating our soup, which unfortunately was not one of my best efforts, but I think Ruth was just thankful to have something to eat. As I got up to get some coffee, I heard a car draw up and realised it was one of the wives from the other night. I dragged Ruth off her chair and up the stairs, motioning her to be quiet. I put her dish and plate in a cupboard, still dirty, and went to the door. I opened it to find a rather large, unattractive woman whom I had labelled as cruel when I met her, but I gave her a bright smile and ushered her in.

"I have brought you some goodies from the mess," she said. "We must make the most of the food whilst it is available."

"Thanks so much. It is good of you to think of Sigmund and me. I do apologise, but I have forgotten your name."

"I'm Ingrid Fischer. Your husband is my husband's boss at the factory. He tells me that the prisoners are lazy and surly, and they stink!"

"I don't suppose they have any facilities to bathe."

"Well, I for one don't give a toss. The less Jews able to work, the more they can get rid of," this hideously spiteful woman said.

"They are human beings after all, Ingrid. How would you like to be treated in such a way?"

"You're not a sympathiser are you, Nicole," said Ingrid, laughing half-heartedly.

"Of course not! Don't be silly. I would not be living here if I was."

I reminded myself that I must be careful what I say. I could give myself away quite easily if I let Ingrid rile me. I saw her studying me whilst she thought I was preoccupied getting coffee ready. We went into the sitting room to have our coffee. The armchairs were luxuriously comfortable, and the room looked out through French doors to a beautiful garden with woodlands beyond.

The malice that Ingrid had was so deep seated that she could not keep from saying, "The Jews certainly knew how to live in comfort."

"They certainly had good taste," I answered non-committedly.

"We will have to have you, Major Fischer, and the rest of the gang round for a meal, so I can use some of the lovely German produce you have brought us from the mess. I thought all the wives could get together and have a competition growing whatever produce we can get seed for. I am trying to get a goat for fresh milk and will have a go at making some goat cheese. I also want to get some chickens. I did get some seeds when I was in town the other day. It is far too cold to start growing at the moment, but there is a greenhouse in the garden: a bit dilapidated, but I will get Sigmund to try to patch it up."

"Oh, Nicole, that would be great. Herman does not think we will be getting supplies for much longer, so we must be as economical as we can. Just don't get started before the rest of us and don't offer me goat milk—I hate the stuff," Ingrid said, screwing up her unattractive face.

I picked up our coffee cups as a hint for Ingrid to leave, and she did not disappointment me. We said good-bye, and she got into what was obviously her husband's staff car, waved, and drove off. I went upstairs into one of the front bedrooms to make sure she had really gone. I waited a few minutes and then knocked on Ruth's bedroom door and entered. I beckoned her to follow me and we went downstairs and into the kitchen.

"If you hear anybody coming or there is a knock at the door, you must hide immediately," I said this slowly, and Ruth at least understood the gist of this and nodded her head.

"Yes," she said.

We had coffee and one of the biscuits that Ingrid had brought with her. I could just imagine her fury if she knew I was sharing the mess food with a Jew. At 6:00 p.m. Sigmund arrived home. Ruth's fear was tangible when she saw him. I put my arms around him and kissed him.

"Hello, darling, this is Ruth."

"Hello, Ruth, I am Sigmund, Nicole's husband, and I will help you all I can. Please do not be frightened."

How much Ruth understood was anyone's guess, but she managed a slight smile and shook Sigmund's hand.

"Ingrid Fischer came round today with some provisions from the mess. She is a despicable person, but I must be more careful when she is castigating the Jews. She asked if I was a sympathiser."

"Darling, you must be more careful. We are playing a dangerous game and must be wary of everyone we are in contact with. We cannot put our trust in anyone."

"I told Ingrid that I would arrange a get together for all those who turned up last time and anyone else you can think of. I also suggested that the wives start to grow vegetables and soft fruit, when the weather improves of course."

"That is a good move. The more normal we act the safer we will be. I have arranged for a girl to come to clean. I don't know her name, but she is not very old, fourteen or fifteen I think. I have arranged for her to stay here, but I must make it look as if she is treated poorly. I thought she could stay in the garage. We can put a bed in there and an electric heater, but she can share with Ruth when no one is around. It will be handy if she can serve the meal when you have your Christmas celebrations. I will also try to get someone to keep the garden under control when spring comes."

We explained to Ruth about the girl coming from the camp and that if anyone was around she would be sleeping in the garage; otherwise, she would be sharing with her. I also explained that I had to go to the church everyday to see if there are messages from the resistance and that she must keep hidden, but the other girl from the camp could be seen as she was officially our cleaner.

Christmas Day fell on a Monday and we decided to have our party on Saturday, 23 December. There would be about twenty people and, of course, the two of us. We knew we could get plenty of drink, and we would have to make do with the food. I sent out the invitations via Sigmund who would hand them out at the factory.

The next morning I went off to the church, but there was no message, so I sat and prayed for a while that we would be successful in our quest to save some of the poor souls barely surviving in the camp. I left the church and went into town to see if there was anything edible to buy. I was able to get some horsemeat to go with the carrots, potatoes, and onions I had at home to make a stew. I thought there were some straggly herbs in the old greenhouse at home to add a bit of flavour.

When I got home, Ruth was hiding in her room. Even after hearing me arrive, she did not check to see whom it was. I called to her, but she did not answer. *Good girl*, I thought—

just the right thing to do. I went up to her room and was greeted with a lovely smile.

"You did very well, Ruth—just what you must always do. Only come down or out of your room if I come and fetch you unless you need the loo, but never even go to the bathroom if you think someone is around. I will put a chamber pot in the cupboard for emergencies."

I found some jigsaws in one of the cupboards, and Ruth had these to occupy her a little. All the books were in Polish, which were of no use to Sigmund or me, but Ruth was able to read them. Although I did my best, our German lessons were very slow as I was not a very good teacher. I got Ruth to help me make the stew, and she seemed happy to do this. While it was cooking, it smelt quite good; however, the proof would be in the eating.

Chapter 23

Sigmund arrived home a little earlier than usual together with a heart-rending specimen of a little girl, clad in the blue-and-white pyjama uniform that all prisoners had to wear. Her tiny pinched face was covered with a mass of sores, and she appeared to be on her last leg. I welcomed her in with a cuddle and Ruth did the same. I then took her to the bathroom, ran her a nice warm and fragrant bath, and set out the smallest clothes I could find that would be warm and comfortable. She was totally bemused, and it would take all our acting skills to make her understand that all we wanted to do was help her. Sigmund put the car in the garage, most unusual, but I soon found out why. He appeared in the kitchen with a little boy, about six or seven years old.

"How did you manage to get him?" I asked incredulously.

"As I was leaving, a trainload of Jews was arriving, and somehow in the chaos I managed to bundle him into the car without anybody seeing. It was mayhem and that helped enormously."

His name turned out to be Jacob, and he was traumatised. Ruth put her arms around him and explained to him in her native tongue that we were there to help him as best we could. We asked her to explain the rules to him that we had explained to her. After giving him a bath, we dressed him in whatever we could find that was not too outrageous.

"I will have to ask around to see if we can get him some proper clothes. I think the priest would be the best bet."

After we had established some semblance of order, it was time for dinner. Ruth laid the table, and our little "skivvy," whose name was Sylvia, helped me dish up, and we all sat down to what turned out to be a reasonable stew. The children ate quickly but mannerly and would have enjoyed food of any kind.

I asked Ruth to explain to the other children that I had to go to the church everyday and if anybody came, Sylvia should be doing something around the house and Jacob and Ruth should remain in silence in their room. Sylvia washed up with the help of Sigmund, who seemed to be smiling all the time, and then sat in the sitting room in front of the fire doing a jigsaw on the floor.

When the children had gone to bed, Sigmund took me in his arms and began to kiss me passionately. Of course as soon as he did so, I was aching for him. We made our way to our room and, for once, had to make love quietly, not an easy task for something so wonderful. Afterward we were lying in each other's arms, and Sigmund turned and looked me straight in the face.

"I can't tell you how wonderful it feels to have the little ones out of that hell hole. I can't wait to do it again and again."

"Sigmund, we have to arrange for Ruth and Jacob to be taken to safety before we get another child, otherwise it is going to be impossible to hide them. In the meantime, do you think we could get some chickens from somewhere so at least we can feed these kids?"

"Ask the priest. He will try to help get them, knowing we have several mouths to feed. I hate this dried milk, so a goat would be a good idea."

The next morning Sigmund left, touching the faces of all three children when he left and, of course, kissing me goodbye while discreetly groping my breast. After eating some bread and jam and drinking a coffee, I rifled round the garden and found some Christmas roses, which I picked to take with me. After warning the children again as to what they had to do should anyone appear in the garden or near the house or knock at the door, I left for the church. It was bitterly cold and snow was falling. I pulled my collar up and wrapped my big woollen scarf around my head and neck and, walking at a pretty fast pace, felt quite warm.

When I arrived at the church, there were two or three women praying, so I set about seeing to the flowers. I went into the vestry to get another vase and found the priest there. I told him about the children and the dilemma regarding clothes for Jacob and Sylvia. I asked if he could get chickens and a goat, and he seemed quite sure that he knew several farmers who would assist me.

"You have three little ones now, Nicole?"

"Well two little ones and Ruth. She can wear my clothes. Sylvia is the 'skivvy' we are allowed to have from the camp, but we will care for her and get her to safety if we possibly can."

I went back out into the main part of the church and the women had gone. There was no message from the resistance, but I left one for them telling them about Jacob and his need to get to safety. I was pretty sure, however, that the priest would tell them as well.

I put a few touches to the flowers, a poor display, and thought about growing some from seed if possible and getting the other wives to do the same. I walked home, head down against the biting wind and sleet. My face felt quite raw by the time I got home. As I entered the house, the smell of bread greeted me. In the kitchen were three very satisfied looking children with broad grins on their faces, and on the table was a small loaf.

"Who made this?" I enquired.

"We all did," said Sylvia. "My grandfather was a baker, and I spent many hours with him in the bakery before the Nazis came."

"You are all very clever and I am grateful, but what if someone came to the house and smelt the bread and realised I was not here?"

"Oh, Nicole, we are really sorry—we did not think," said Ruth.

"There is nothing to be sorry about, but I must keep you safe, and simple things like this could give you away," I said giving each one a hug.

We spent the rest of the day having German lessons—a very trying time for us all, and an English lesson, which was far better as they had been taught English at school before the Nazi invasion of Poland; even little Jacob knew a little. We looked through the larder to see what we could find and discovered tins of meat in gravy and some rather withered looking vegetables, but we put them all in a large pot and simmered them. I had no idea what the meat was, but if we cooked it well, it would do us no harm. We added herbs and a little suet and made small dumplings.

Sigmund came home at 6:00 p.m., pale and distraught looking. We kissed, and he patted all the children on their heads. I knew not to ask questions in front of the children. They had seen and heard enough horrendous happenings. The sound of a loud vehicle could be heard coming up the lane, and I feared it was a tank. The children ran upstairs, and Sigmund went out to see what it was. I heard a brief but friendly conversation and then the noise going back down the lane. Sigmund came into the kitchen with two chickens and a few clothes for Jacob.

"Crikey, I only asked the priest for these this morning. Who was it?"

"It was one of the farmers from the other side of the woods, and he hoped they could be of use," Sigmund answered.

"We will have to keep the chickens in the garage in case of foxes. The farmer gave us a small amount of grain for them, but he said during the day they will just forage in the garden for food."

"What happens to me when I sleep in the garage? Will the chickens be with me?" Sylvia asked.

"Yes, but there should not be too many occasions when that happens," Sigmund told her.

"I don't mind," Sylvia said genuinely.

When we went to bed, I asked Sigmund why he was in such a state when he came home.

"Darling, they have increased the number of exterminations in No. 1 Auschwitz. I had to go there this morning and saw lines of naked men, women, children, and babies waiting to be gassed. They have killed so many that they can't burn them quickly enough, and there are piles of emaciated bodies just lying around. It is indescribable."

"You poor darling. I cannot even begin to imagine the horror."

Sigmund was watery eyed and once we were in bed I held him tight as he sobbed into his pillow, such heartrending sounds that I, too, started to sob.

"We must try to help more, darling. It is the only thing we can do against the power of the Nazis."

"Darling, I'm so ashamed to be one of them and not have the guts to speak out."

"Sigmund, you would be executed as a traitor if you did. We are helping, if only in a small way."

The next day before he left for work I asked if he had distributed the invitations to our Christmas party. He said yes and that everyone was coming.

"Goodness knows what we are going to feed them."

"I'll get something from the mess," he said as he kissed me good-bye.

The children had their breakfast, and I went off to the church as usual, with the normal warnings to them about hiding if anyone came, apart from Sylvia. I was surprised and pleased to find a message saying that the resistance would be at our pre-arranged rendezvous. Both Ruth and Jacob were to go with them for onward transit to safety, please God.

I fiddled with the flowers just in case anyone was watching, adding some holly to the arrangements, if you could call them that, but they were better than nothing. I went into the town square and bought a few bits and pieces, anything that was available. I then walked home, stopping to chat with one of the other wives who told me how much they were looking forward to the twenty-third.

"If you have any titbits you could bring, we would be grateful. We have plenty of booze but, as you know, food is in short supply."

"I will bring anything I have suitable. Well I'll see you then, Nicole. Bye for now."

When I got home, I called the children together and told them that both Ruth and Jacob would be going tonight. I explained to Sylvia that once Sigmund got another girl of similar stature, she would be going too, but I did not know exactly when.

That night, 16 December at 2:00 a.m., I led Ruth and Jacob, wrapped up warmly against the extreme cold, through the garden and into the disused causeway that went all the way to the other side of Auschwitz. It was hard going as the ground was uneven and the snow had drifted in places, which made it deep and difficult to get through. At last we arrived at the rendezvous. Nobody spoke a word. I kissed the children and left immediately to return home whilst the rest of them went in the opposite direction to their next rendezvous. It was even harder getting back as there was a heavy blizzard, but at least it would cover our footsteps.

I got back at 3:15 a.m. to a joyous Sigmund and Sylvia who had refused to go to bed until I was home safely. Sylvia hugged me hard and had a huge smile on her tiny face.

"Off to bed with you," I said.

Sigmund and I went to bed also and made love for quite a while, stopping when we were near climaxing to make it last as long as possible. We came together in many positions but obviously it had to end.

"I love you, Nicole. I was so worried whilst you were gone."

"I love you too, Sigmund, more than I thought it possible to love anyone. We have started our mission, and I can't wait until we get another prisoner or even more to safety. I have told Sylvia that once you get another girl from the camp, we will get her to the resistance and, hopefully, to safety. Having their heads shaved helps because it make them look more alike." We dropped off and had a deep, if short, sleep.

Apart from Sigmund having to cope with the terrible events at the camps, the next few days were uneventful. I had no messages at the church or any conversations with the priest. On 19 December, when Sigmund came home, he drove into the garage. He came in through the integral door to make sure we had no visitors and then brought two little ones into the kitchen wearing the usual pyjamas and looking dirty, hungry, and terrified. I went to them and put my arms round them. I was not sure what sex they were until Sigmund enlightened me that they were girls. Sylvia explained to them what was going on, and they looked at Sigmund and me in wonder. Sylvia also told them the important rules that had to be obeyed to the letter for everyone's safety and that one day fairly soon they would be taken to safety.

Sylvia enjoyed getting things ready for our Christmas get together on 23 December although she knew she would be in the garage with the chickens and back in her blue-and-white prison attire whilst waiting on the Nazis. Sylvia understood, too, that Sigmund and I would not be overly friendly towards her. Our guests knew she was here to work as if she was in the camp. I hoped nobody would be too unkind to her.

The two new girls, Ada and Felisberta Muller, had settled in well. They were ten and eleven, and Felisberta was the oldest. Both were so happy to be away from the horrors of the concentration camp and had several marks on them caused by physical abuse. I was pretty sure they had been sexually assaulted, but they did not confirm this. They knew that whilst we had the party they too would be in the garage, but in the loft just in case anybody wandered in.

Felisberta showed me how to make boiled eggs, take out the yolk, mix it with chopped gherkins, and return the mixture to the white. Then the eggs could be covered with grated cheese and grilled. They looked very good and were attractive. We had been fortunate with the chickens and had two eggs on most days. I asked Sylvia if she could make some of the delicious bread that they had made before, and she was delighted to do this for me.

"I don't want you to feel bad about making food for these people, especially the ones that you had contact with in the camp. Just tell yourself that they are terrible people who are treating prisoners cruelly, and by feeding them, you are so much better than they are."

"I am still alive, Nicole, and I have you and Sigmund to thank while thousands are not. I would do anything for you."

On my daily visits to the church, I found no messages, but the priest did get clothes for Ada and Felisberta. The girls had all helped me make holly wreaths and crosses as decorations for the church, and I had collected some thistle heads, which we decorated with paint from a children's paint box that we found amongst the things in the house. They were really rather pretty, and the priest said how nice I had made the church look.

"My girls did most of the work and thoroughly enjoyed making them. Would you like to come to our house on 23 December? I think that some of those who are going to attend come to your church."

"I don't think so, but thank you, Nicole."

Before I left, I wrote a message telling the resistance that we had two more little ones to get to safety.

On the day of our party, the invited guests arrived even though the weather was atrocious. Sylvia took their coats whilst being completely ignored. The awful Ingrid and Ada virtually threw their coats at her, hoping she would drop them so she could be chastised. Her little face did not move a muscle, and she did not look them in the eye as this would have been deemed unseemly.

The evening went very well; lots of booze was consumed and all the food went. The bread was a great success as were the stuffed eggs. Our guests would probably have choked on them if they knew who had made them. Several times fingers were snapped at Sylvia for her to get drinks and pass plates but, bless her, she made no sign of being intimidated.

Ingrid came over to me and asked loudly, "Where does she sleep?" The other Sylvia sidled up to hear my answer.

"In the garage with the chickens. Why?" I answered.

"I couldn't bear the thought that she slept in the house, a prisoner from the camp, yuk!" Ingrid said, never knowing when to stop.

I ignored her last remark and went over to Sigmund and put my arms around him, just to reassure myself that I must not retaliate in any way. Ingrid and Ada and their respective spouses got louder and louder the more they drank and so did a couple of others, but I could not for the life of me remember their names, and I certainly wasn't going to ask.

I wondered how the two little girls were getting on in the garage loft. They had plenty of warm blankets, but I wished our visitors would leave.

"Are you going to show us your chickens, Nicole?"

"Not at this time of night, I'm not. If they got out, we would not be able to catch them and the foxes might get them."

At last the couples began to ready themselves for their homeward journeys. Coats were donned, large woolly scarves were wrapped round their heads and shoulders, and they all bent double running to their cars. The last couple finally left, Ingrid and her husband. I was beginning not to trust her.

"Don't forget the vegetable growing competition, Ingrid," I called after her. "We should be able to get some seeds after Christmas."

Ingrid gave me the thumbs up as she fell into the car, laughing raucously. Sigmund shut the door with a sigh of relief.

"Thank goodness they have gone. What an evil piece of work that Ingrid is—mind you, I don't think Ada is any better."

"Are you all right, Sylvia? I am sorry they were so horrible. If you don't mind, I think you should sleep in the garage as well as Ada and Felisberta, in case they come back if the snow is too deep," I put my arms round her and squeezed her tightly.

"Of course I don't mind. I was going to suggest it as that woman was very interested in where I slept," Sylvia said seriously.

Sigmund insisted on escorting Sylvia to the garage through the integral door. He called up to Ada and Felisberta to see if they were all right. Getting no answer, he climbed the ladder and lifted the loft cover. They were both sound asleep, wrapped warmly and cuddled up together. Sigmund lowered the cover, put the ladder back against the far wall, and made sure Sylvia had enough blankets. We had found a stone hot-water bottle, which she had wrapped in a scarf for an extra bit of warmth. Sigmund gave her a hug, made sure the external door of the garage was locked, and came back in through the integral door.

I had cleaned up the rest of the bits and pieces—Sylvia had done most of it as the evening progressed, and I was in the bedroom getting ready for bed. Sigmund came up behind me and cupped my breasts in his hands, nuzzling my neck and then turning me round and kissing me tenderly.

"You did so well tonight. What an obnoxious bunch they are."

"I was so afraid I was going to have a go at Ingrid. I don't like her interest in Sylvia, and I certainly don't trust her," I said. "I would not have been surprised if she had come back tonight to see if Sylvia was actually sleeping in the garage."

"It went through my mind too, but I locked the garage door from the inside just in case."

We got into bed and had our usual session of passionate lovemaking; it was getting better and better.

Chapter 24

We had a peaceful Christmas. Sigmund and I went to church Christmas Day, struggling through the snow and biting wind. It proved very worthwhile, as I had a message that Ada and Felisberta would be going with the resistance the night of 27 December. Both Sigmund and I were elated that our small contribution to saving prisoners was working, although we knew we must never be complacent. We still had to get the girls to the church safely. Going home was easier with the wind at our backs. I had left a chicken in the oven, not one of ours but a gift from a farmer via the priest, and Sylvia was keeping an eye on it and looking forward to us all having dinner together.

We told the girls when they would be leaving and reminded Sylvia that she would be going as soon as we had a replacement for her. Sigmund said it was tricky finding a girl of similar appearance, age, and one who would not be missed.

Boxing Day was spent with the girls reading and me making chicken soup for dinner and baking bread, supervised by Sylvia. Sigmund got up and went to the window. "Go to your room girls and be completely silent. We have visitors." Ada and Felisberta dashed upstairs and into their room.

"Oh Lord, it's that awful Ingrid and her husband," said Sigmund as he went to open the front door.

"Surprise! We thought we would come for a short visit as it is too cold to go for a walk, which is what we intended. What a lovely smell, Nicole, are you making bread again," said Ingrid hopefully.

"Yes I am, but I did not have enough ingredients and it is very small, so I am afraid I cannot offer you any." I felt so smug saying this when I saw a flash of annoyance in Ingrid's eyes. "I can offer you coffee and a biscuit though."

We went into the sitting room where the fire was burning well with logs from the woods. Sigmund and Ingrid's husband were discussing the Eastern Front, the massive loss of life on both sides, and the dreadful treatment of the Russian prisoners of war. Apparently they were being starved to death. The German troops did not have suitable clothing or enough food. Ingrid was waffling on, talking away, but I managed to close my ears to most of her conversation until she started to talk about our plan for the vegetable competition.

"I have managed to get some packets of seeds—carrots, cabbage, lettuce, and tomatoes."

"Where did you get them?" I asked jealously.

"That would be telling, but I hope to get a head start and win." Ingrid smiled as she answered, but I knew she meant it.

"Well, my dear, I think we should be going now," Ingrid said, and her husband got up. Sigmund got their coats and wraps, and they went on their merry way.

"I think she only came to brag about her seeds. I would love to know where she got them. I am jealous. I don't want her to win." Sigmund laughed as I went upstairs to get the girls.

When we were together in the sitting room, I explained to Ada and Felisberta that it was important they eat as much as they could as it may be some time before the resistance got them to their next destination.

"Do you know where we are going?" asked Ada worriedly.

"No, my love, I am afraid I don't. We don't tell each other details, so that if we get caught we cannot give away any secrets."

I went into the kitchen to concoct as nourishing a meal as I could. We still had some eggs, and soup, not very tasty but fairly nutritious, fresh bread that Sylvia had made, and potatoes. I peeled lots of potatoes, filling and full of carbohydrates, and mashed them up with a small piece of grated cheese and milk. I then baked them. We ended up with a large piece of potato cake, an omelette, and soup. I opened a tin of peaches that came from the mess that was so large it would do us for many days. Sigmund and I made sure that the girls had plenty to eat, and I found an assortment of clothes that they could layer for their journey that night—or rather early in the morning. At least it was not snowing, but it was freezing and would be very hard going, especially in the gully that would be slippery under the snow.

"Would you like to try and have a sleep?" Sigmund asked Ada and Felisberta.

Felisberta said she did not think she could sleep, so we sat round trying to be as cheerful as we could without showing our apprehension.

At 2:00 a.m. the girls dressed as warmly as they could and looked at least two sizes larger than they were. I also dressed warmly and wore a cape over my coat that was light in colour and would not stand out against the snow too much. We set off, leaving Sigmund and Sylvia with anxious faces at the door. It was cloudy and so hard to see our way, but I dared not use a light. We slipped and fell several times, and I was sure we were behind time. When we got to the rendezvous point, no one was there. I pushed the girls into the cover of the trees, putting my finger to my lips. About five minutes later two men appeared.

One of them whispered, "We thought you had been held up or caught!"

"The going was difficult. I'm sorry we are late."

The man patted me on the shoulder. I kissed the girls, and they disappeared into the darkness in the care of the resistance. I turned and got back down in the gully. As I made my way slowly through the ice and snow, I slipped on something under the snow. When I went down, I knew I had hurt my ankle and was unable to put any weight on it when I tried to stand. I decided the best thing to do was crawl, as I did not want to be laid up and incapable of doing the escape run for a while. Hence, I was delayed getting back. Sigmund was beside himself with worry, but Sylvia was sound asleep on the couch. I am sure she wanted to stay awake but was unable to do so.

"Darling, I think we must give this a rest for a while, even after your ankle has healed. It is getting more and more dangerous." Sigmund looked into my eyes and kissed me. "Let me see to your ankle."

He examined my ankle and twisted it this way and that. It was painful and swollen but not broken. I soaked it in a bowl of hot, salted water, my mother's cure for most things, after which I sat in the armchair with my foot raised on a stool and covered in a blanket. I fell into a deep sleep.

Sigmund had to go to the factory on the twenty-eighth and was gone long before I awakened. Dear little Sylvia was sitting watching over me and as soon as I was awake, she got me a coffee and a slice of bread to dip in it. I didn't know what we would do when the coffee ran out. This was a luxury and a gift from Ingrid who had gotten it from the mess. I told Sylvia to have one as well, but she preferred a glass of powdered milk.

We must really get her away to safety, I thought. I could not put any weight on my ankle, so Sigmund had gone to the church to leave a message for the resistance or the priest, making them aware of my predicament and telling them that we wanted to get Sylvia out. If the resistance agreed to get her out, we would report her missing once she had been gone for a few days. Whether or not we would get a replacement, we did not know. If we did not, Sigmund would have to try to get the prisoners away by any means he could. This, of course, was going to be extremely difficult and dangerous for Sigmund and the prisoners.

Later that day Ingrid and her friend Ada arrived, having been told of my fall. Actually I was glad they came, because they topped up our supplies of sugar, flour, dried egg, powdered milk, tins of lard, and dried sausages. Sylvia was very subservient, and they were not too unpleasant to her.

"How did you do this?" Ada asked, holding my ankle in her hands and gently manipulating it.

"I slipped in the yard where the snow had covered the ice."

"I don't think it is too bad," Ada went on. "I used to be a nurse, and I am sure the best thing is to use it as much as possible, inside of course. You don't want to slip again."

"Thank you, Ada, I will take your advice," I said sweetly.

They stayed for about an hour and then left. Ingrid mistakenly went through the integral garage door; luckily, we always kept the bed covered with old sheets and blankets as though it was in permanent use. Of course, she meant to do this but apologised profusely. *What a cow*, I thought, *she is checking up on me.*

When Sigmund got home after visiting the church, I told him of Ingrid's escapade and said I thought she was checking that I was not being too kind to Sylvia—our own little Sylvia of course.

"I saw the priest and he said that Sylvia can go on 30 December, the same time as the others, about 2:30 a.m. All the others have made it through as far as they know, but they want a break after Sylvia. They have several families in dire need of help that are not Jews but have been accused of various crimes, all fictitious."

"Oh, Sylvia will be so pleased. That's only about thirty-six hours away. I must exercise my ankle as much as possible," I said as I hugged him.

"I will take her, darling. You are not fit."

"No, you will not!" I answered him emphatically. "I definitely am going myself and absolutely insist on it. I will stay at the church once Sylvia has gone and come back later in the morning, as though I have just been there to sort the flowers and visit the shops."

The following day, I managed to go to the church despite considerable pain in my ankle, but I knew it was best to use it as much as possible. I managed to buy flowers in town, four roses and a few chrysanthemums, goodness knows where they came from. I did my usual arrangements, and after I finished, a well-to-do-looking woman approached me.

"I notice that you have injured your ankle. Perhaps I can give you a lift home, Nicole."

"I'm sorry, but you are ahead of me. I do not know your name, but you somehow know mine."

"Good turns deserve rewards. I know you have carried out numerous good deeds, and I would like to assist you in any way I can."

"May I know your name and how you know of me?"

"Of course. My name is Polinski, Sara Polinski, and I know of you through your work with the resistance wherever you have been. You are very brave and a heroine in many people's opinion. I am a friend, Nicole, a safe friend."

At that moment the priest came out of the vestry, nodded to us, and actually gave me the thumbs up.

"I would greatly appreciate a lift home, Sara. Perhaps you would like to come in for coffee. I would be grateful for a friend. Apart from my husband, I have no one I can trust, and I think the wife of one of the officers is suspicious that I may be sympathetic to Jews."

"As proof of my genuine wish to be a friend to you, I am confiding in you that I am a Jew."

Sara and I left the church, and I got into her beautiful and expensive car. When we reached my house, she seemed pleased that it was secluded. Sara followed me into the house, and I introduced her to Sylvia.

"Is this the little one going tomorrow?"

"Yes, and I will miss her very much. She is a lovely girl." Sylvia was smiling broadly, looking quite proud.

"It has been suggested that I take Sylvia back with me today and get her to the rendezvous tomorrow night, if that is all right with you and your husband."

"If it is all right with Sylvia, then I agree. It would be much safer if you take her to your house and then to the rendezvous. We will report her missing in four days, by which time she should be well on her way. We don't think the Nazis will conduct much of a search for her. We will report that Sylvia was wearing the thin cotton pyjamas that was the outfit that she wore constantly. She will be without a coat and wearing tatty shoes, and the weather is bitter."

"What do you think, Sylvia, are you happy to do this?" asked Sara kindly.

"If Nicole thinks it is all right, then I am happy to go with you."

Believe it or not, a car came up the lane and into our drive. It was Ingrid of course. Sylvia opened the door and Ingrid swept in.

"Why are you not in your prisoner's garb?" she asked Sylvia spitefully.

"It is in the wash. I could not stand the smell of it any longer," I answered. "I don't think it has anything to do with you in any case."

Sara jumped in holding out her hand to Ingrid. "Hi, I'm Sara, a friend to Nicole. Pleased to meet you."

Ingrid beamed at Sara, taking in her expensive clothing and jewellery. "I'm Ingrid and also a friend to Nicole. I popped in to see how her ankle is. My friend Ada looked at it yesterday and thought it was just a slight sprain and that she should use it as much as possible."

"Of course, but whether it should be rested or not depends on the severity of the sprain," said Sara. "My husband is a doctor and is home on leave from the Medical Corps, so I will ask him to come to see Nicole tomorrow."

"Perhaps you and your husband would like to come to dinner some evening if you are free."

Ingrid was determined to ingratiate herself to Sara, but I could tell from Sara's face that she was in no way going to become friends with this awful woman.

"Maybe, one day, but not in the near future, as my husband is shortly returning to the Eastern Front."

Ingrid could not hide her disappointment. She said she had other calls to make and went to her car, obviously in a huff.

"I don't know how she gets her husband's staff car so often. I thought that was a no no," I said.

After we had a good old chinwag about the war and the terrible atrocities being carried out by the Nazis, Sara looked at her watch.

"I think I should be making a move. My husband will come to see you tomorrow to check your ankle and to meet you. He also is very impressed with your bravery and your work with the resistance in France and now in Poland."

Sylvia was dressed warmly in clothes donated by someone from the church and looked apprehensive. I cuddled her and said, "Good-bye, my darling. I pray that God will keep you safe throughout your journey and for the rest of your life."

Sylvia kissed and hugged me as though she would not let me go. "Thank you, Nicole, for all you and Sigmund have done for me. I hope you don't get into trouble."

Sara took her hand and led her to the car where she put her in the boot, made comfortable by an eiderdown for her to lie on. Sara got into her car. "See you soon," she said. Her car hardly made a sound as she drove off with her precious cargo.

When Sigmund came home, I told him of the events of the day and that Sylvia had already gone.

"I'm sorry not to have said good-bye but glad that you did not have to risk taking her to the rendezvous. We will leave it for as long as possible before reporting her missing. I have been posted to the Eastern Front, where there is a shortage of soldiers due to the extreme cold and the vicious fighting. Apparently the Russians have been under siege for a long time with no food but are continuing to fight as hard as ever. I can have a week's leave before I go, so we can spend the whole time making love." Sigmund's eyes were sparkling as he said this. "I am due to go on 5 January."

"That is only six days away. I really don't want you to go, but I know how you feel about Auschwitz. I will find somewhere else to live, so I can carry on what we have started. I will ask Sara if she knows of a place I can rent cheaply. I only need a small place while on my own." "Promise me that you will not put yourself in danger my darling."

"Sigmund, you know that is a promise I cannot keep. I might even go back to Blois if I'm needed there. The Polish resistance will know where I can be of most use, and if I go back home, I might even get a job at the Chateau again. Sara's husband is coming tomorrow to look at my ankle. He is a medic and home on leave."

For most of the evening, we curled up together on the couch in front of the fire and talked about the small number of people that we had helped to save. We both felt sorry that we had not been able to save more, but at least we had tried our best. Sigmund had his arms around me pulling me close, and I could feel his hardness.

"Let's go to bed," he said. Of course, I had no objections. Our lovemaking was long and tender, but we both thought of our parting.

In the morning Sigmund was getting in wood for the fire when Sara's husband, Pietre, arrived. I watched them as they shook hands, and I was pretty sure he was as sympathetic as Sigmund towards those being persecuted. They came in together, and after Pietre checked my ankle and confirmed that it was better to use it as much as I could to stop it from stiffening, he asked if we would like to go to their home on New Year's Eve.

"Sara is having a small get together and would be delighted if you would come."

"Thank you Pietre, that would be wonderful. You must give us directions, as I haven't a clue where you live," I said.

"Better still, I will come and pick you up. Sara would never forgive me if you got lost and did not turn up."

After I thanked Pietre for coming, both he and Sigmund went outside and Sigmund stood admiring Pietre's car. They must be well heeled, as this was a different car from the one Sara drove. They were laughing together, completely at ease in each other's company, and I felt so glad that Sigmund had someone with his own principles, or so I hoped.

I wrapped up warmly to go to the church, to keep to my routine, and Sigmund decided to come with me. Time seemed to be flying by, and we wanted to be with each other as much as we could. It still was fairly hard going as my ankle was painful and the snow was covering several patches of ice causing us to slip and slide and cling to each other laughing. No one was in the church and I had not been able to find any flowers, so I just tidied up the ones that were still alive and threw the drooping and dead ones away.

When we got home I asked, "What are you going to wear tonight to Sara and Pietre's party?"

"My dress uniform, of course. Pietre made a point of asking me to do so. What about you?"

"I think I will wear my long, silk, emerald-green dress, as I have not had a chance to dress up for yonks."

"Oh heck. I won't be able to keep my hands off you if you wear that dress."

"What a shame, you will just have to remember that we are in company." I laughed.

"Might be able to manage a little grope though," Sigmund teased.

As promised Pietre arrived in his luxurious car looking handsome in his dress uniform, but definitely not as gorgeous as my man. The drive was difficult as the snow was coming down heavily, but we arrived at their home safe and sound. It was magnificent and stood at the end of a long drive. Even with no lights showing, in case of air raids, it oozed wealth.

The inside was just as spectacular, full of antique furniture and wonderful paintings and ornaments.

"Wow, this is some place," I said to Sara. "I'm green with envy."

"It is inherited. My great-great-grandfather purchased it originally. He was an art dealer, hence many of the beautiful pictures. Our precious cargo got away safely."

"Thank you for helping, Sara. It was a relief that I did not have to trudge through the snow with my sore ankle."

Sara introduced us to the rest of the guests. I was greatly surprised that they were all SS officers and their wives. They were all friendly, and Sigmund even knew one or two of them. The discussion got round to the Eastern Front, and it turned out that most of them were on leave prior to going there. The evening was lovely, but there was a bitter sweet atmosphere as most of our husbands were off to the front where we knew fierce fighting and cold was taking a heavy toll on German lives. Completely under siege, Russians, both civilians and soldiers alike, were suffering greatly.

"It is rumoured," said a very young officer, "that they are having to eat dead bodies to stay alive. What a terrible thing war is. Still, we all go along with our orders without question."

"There have been a few attempts to assassinate Hitler, but none have been successful and those concerned in the attempts have been executed," answered Pietre. "I would dearly love a chance myself."

The rest of the men said a genuine, "Here, here."

I realised that all the people attending this get together were not sympathetic to Hitler or his regime, and I am certain if they were to be stationed together they would probably try to overthrow Hitler.

After a few drinks, the atmosphere got lighter and jokes were told, some rude, some downright disgusting, and some derogatory to Hitler. We were crying with laughter especially when Pietre told his jokes. His repertoire seemed endless and my sides literally ached with laughter.

We saw the New Year in, and we all wondered if we would be here for the next one. Everyone started to leave and Pietre went to get the car to take us home.

Sara held my arm and said, "You and I can do our bit too, can't we? There are plenty of people still hiding and hoards being brought from France and Germany for extermination."

"Yes, of course, Sara. I have a little house in Blois, France and we could go there, if we are needed."

We embraced and said we would be in touch once the boys had gone. Until then, we wanted to spend as much time alone with our husbands. Sigmund was true to his word and groped me whilst kissing me at the turn of midnight.

Chapter 25

The fifth of January came so quickly, and Sigmund and I were clinging to each other for dear life when it was time for him to go.

"Take care, my darling. Please come home to me and write if you are able."

"Nicole, you too, must take care. I know that you and Sara are planning to carry on helping the resistance, but you will be watched more closely when I'm gone. You know that Ingrid is a troublemaker and you must appear squeaky clean. I love you with all my heart and soul, my dearest, dearest girl."

I started to cry, a thing I had promised not to do because I wanted Sigmund to have a memory of me waving good-bye and smiling. Sigmund's eyes were watery, and he gave me one last kiss and left, waving and blowing kisses as he drove off. I wondered if I would see him again.

On 6 January 1942, I reported Sylvia missing, saying that she had gone the previous evening when we were both preoccupied with Sigmund's departure. The commandant at the camp asked what Sylvia was wearing, and I told him she was wearing the thin blue-and-white striped uniform and tatty shoes and that she had left the outfit that we had given her behind.

"Oh well, she will probably die from exposure, so we won't worry too much about finding her. I will order soldiers to shoot her if they come across her on their patrols."

Bastard! I thought to myself. He would really like that to happen. He looked decidedly cruel when he gave me a false smile.

When I got home, Sara arrived and we sat down and began to plot our next move.

"I reported Sylvia missing this morning," I said.

"Did they offer you another girl?" Sara enquired.

"No. The commandant is a cruel man and has told his soldiers to shoot her on sight if they see Sylvia. I don't think he would risk me having another girl to lose. He would rather exterminate her for his own pleasure."

"I have arranged a meeting with the resistance for this evening so we can get cracking. They will meet us in the vestry, so if you come home with me now, we can go from my house to the church. I have some flowers that you can take as a guise, in case there is someone in the church. I will be going to pray."

The priest was alone, and we went straight into the vestry where two Poles were waiting. They looked worn out and hungry. Sara must have second sense because she had brought several items of food with her, which she gave them to their obvious delight and relief.

"We need someone to be taken to a rendezvous fairly quickly. It is on the border between Poland and Slovakia so it is quite a journey, about two hundred and thirty-nine kilometres. They are going behind enemy lines to send information back. Terrible atrocities are being reported, and they want to see if there is an active resistance."

"There is very heavy fighting throughout Poland, through which we will have to drive, and we are quite likely to be stopped," Sara said.

One of the men spoke. "We have a cover story that a relative of yours is sick and quite likely to die and wants to see you. The fact that you are both married to German SS officers should stand you in good stead if you are stopped, but the bombing is heavy and a credible hazard. As stated before, none of us ever knows the names of the resistance members."

"We are hoping that a Slav will be there to come back with you if he has survived his mission," said the younger of the two, who had not spoken before apart from saying hello. "We have not heard from him for quite a while but, of course, that may be of no significance. I hope not anyway, we all do."

The two men gave us a paper with reference points, emphasising that it must be destroyed after we had digested the route and said their farewells. The priest blessed them and wished them God's protection at all times. The priest then blessed Sara and me, and we set off for Sara's home to check the route we had to take and collect our overnight bags as if we were indeed going to visit an ailing relative. The route given to us seemed to be fraught with danger. Bombing raids and heavy land fighting were our main concerns, but Sara, a source of constant solutions, knew of a country route that, hopefully would give us some chance of a successful mission.

Chapter 26

We left Sara's house and set off, luckily with enough petrol for the return journey courtesy of the SS. We had a thermos of coffee and some biscuits. We picked up our fellow traveller who had to go in the boot, which Sara had lined with a heavily filled eiderdown to make him more comfortable. We had not gone more than twenty kilometres when a raid started. We parked the car as best we could under cover and found a hiding place away from buildings and making sure there were no patrols about before letting our companion out.

The Luftwaffe was active until daybreak, so we had to stay hidden all night. The noise from the bombs had been deafening and made the Earth shake after one dropped about half a mile away. It permeated the air with the smell of explosives. We had both been frightened and were glad when it became calm, at least for the time being. We had a cup of our coffee and tried to relax.

We got in the car and continued on our journey. During the time we were hiding, our companion had not said a word. Shortly after starting out we were stopped at a checkpoint and communicated this to the person in the boot. I hoped he felt calmer than I did. The soldiers were belligerent until they saw our papers and changed their attitudes greatly. They did not ask to see inside the car, thank goodness. They asked where we were going and said we must be on our guard at all times as the resistance was active, and the allies were carrying out bombing raids. In fact, Germans, trying to destroy the spirit of the Poles, had flown the planes we heard last night.

As we left the checkpoint, Sara said, "Seeing their arrogance and knowing that they are slaughtering so many people without giving two hoots makes you want to slap their faces. Seeing our papers and our husband's names soon changed their tune. I wonder if Sigmund and Pietre managed to meet any like minds. It would be wonderful if they could get rid of Hitler, but I don't suppose he will put himself at risk and visit the Eastern Front. I wonder how they are and how long it will be until we get news from them, or from someone else on the front who comes home on leave."

Sara patted my knee when she heard the wobble in my voice as I spoke of Sigmund. "Mind you, we have to carry out this mission safely, otherwise we will not be around to get any news."

If all went well, we should make the border by late afternoon. We could hear the noise of an aircraft nearby. It did not sound like a bomber but was probably on a recognisance mission following last night's bombing raid. We kept going and about lunchtime came across another checkpoint. We were treated in the same brusque manner, and this did not change when we showed them our papers. The soldier who appeared to be in charge lifted the phone and confirmed the names of Sigmund and Pietre. Satisfied that our papers were in order, he waved us on our way. Thankfully, once again they made no attempt to check the car. We stopped to finish the coffee, unfortunately now cold; it wet our whistles, and we finished the biscuits.

"We may find a baker in one of the villages as we are in a very rural area," Sara said hopefully. I smiled at her.

"That would be nice, a lovely fresh piece of bread, hot out of the oven."

"Stop it. You are making me salivate. My stomach is beginning to rebel."

Sara's stomach was churning away probably because she was more used to good fare than me. We did not find a baker, but we found a farm and bought milk, butter, and cheese.

"Have you any bread to spare?" Sara enquired sweetly.

The farmer's wife, or daughter for that matter, sold us a piece of breadstick. I think she was wondering what a well-to-do German woman in a posh car was doing on a rural road asking for food.

We only went about a mile before we stopped and drank some milk and ate some bread and cheese. Luckily, Sara had a nail file (clean of course) and we were able to spread the butter crudely on the bread and break the cheese with our fingers. It tasted wonderful. We shared the bottle of milk, which was creamy and fresh, and our companion smiled and thanked us.

It was dark by 4:30 p.m. when we approached our designated meeting place. We drove around a little to make sure the coast was clear and then went back to the place we had been told to go. We stopped the engine and sat for a while. The back door of the car opened and two men got in.

"Have you got our package?" asked the elder of the two, the other a seemingly young man.

"Yes, in the boot," answered Sara. "We were stopped twice, but the boot was not checked. I will have to find another route back and not for at least another day as our cover is that we are visiting a dying relative."

"We could perhaps make a space under the back seat for your return journey. The man concerned is young and fit and can manage any conditions." The man directed us to drive into a large, empty, barn-like construction. "You can stay here until you think it prudent to start back on your return journey. There is wine and homemade bread and a jar of preserved fruit to tide you over until you get back home—safely I hope. I am sorry there is so little, but as you can imagine, we are very short of food."

Our travelling companion went off without a word and was replaced by the young man as our companion.

The two of them lifted up the back seat, which came up quite easily revealing quite a good space, not as good as the boot but obviously safer.

"I may be able to make some sort of false floor out of plywood that will cover him. If the SS stop you and lift the seat, it will appear to be empty if not scrutinised too closely."

"Thank you," Sara said, and we both went and sat on some boxes and had a glass of wine, which was very palatable.

"What concerns me is whether there be will be enough air getting in for him, and what about the exhaust fumes?" Sara asked thoughtfully.

"We will drill holes in the top of the seats, which will be hidden in the ridges of the leather. These holes will go undetected and should let in enough ventilation. You could open your windows as much as possible and that will also help with his airflow," the older man said. "You will have to wrap up warmly. The weather is still bitterly cold. It must have been very difficult for you with all this snow and the back roads you took to get here.

We are all very grateful for what you are doing and have done to help with the escapes from Auschwitz."

Neither Sara nor I made any comment. We have always been taught to be discreet, and we certainly did not want to drop Sigmund or Pietre into the equation regarding the escapes from Auschwitz. Just thinking of Sigmund made me ache for him.

"I wonder how our boys are getting on," I said to Sara with watery eyes.

"I hope they are safe. I know the fighting is fierce and the conditions dire," Sara said sadly.

"War is such a terrible thing. It would be wonderful if Hitler could be assassinated," I replied.

Sara made no comment as we sat silently for a while, drinking our wine and eating the preserved fruit, rather messy eating as we had no cutlery. The large plums, cooked with some sort of herb added to the syrupy water, were very tasty. As we enjoyed our snack, the men got on with working on the back seat of the car. I think Sara was rather worried about how much damage might be done to her beautiful car, but we both knew that this was the best option. Later, the younger of the two men went out the back of the building and came back with blankets and cushions for us to sleep on. They continued working on the car throughout the night. It was noisy to say the least, but we both dropped off now and again. Luckily, there was a toilet and hand basin out the back so we were able to have a wash in the morning.

"Would it be possible for you to get us some food to see us through the day? I know provisions are hard to come by, but we need to have something in our stomachs for the journey home. I intend leaving around eight tomorrow morning if the car is ready," Sara said.

"The car will be ready, and my wife is making a goulash out of what I don't know, but it is always tasty," the elder gentleman said, still working away.

The day dragged by. We had brought a couple of books to read, but it was difficult to concentrate. Sara was anxiously trying to plan a new route home but had to take into account the snow and ice. We did not want to get marooned and draw attention to ourselves.

"Nicole, I think we will go back on the main road. Our papers are in order as is our alibi, and I think the risk might be higher on back roads. That farmer's wife seemed rather interested in us."

"I think that is a good idea. If we had been visiting a dying relative, I don't think we would be on back roads, especially when the relative has died. We would want to get home as soon as possible," I answered.

"Come and see," the man called, and we went over to the car.

He had done an amazing job. The younger man got into the bottom of the back seat and a plywood cover was put over him that rested on ledges to hold it in place. He appeared to have enough room, and the older man put the seat down.

"Can you start the car so we can check the fumes, please?"

"Of course," said Sara, getting into the car and starting the engine. Sara revved the engine and ran it for quite a while.

"That seems all right. I told the lad to knock if there was any seepage."

Chapter 27

Just before eight the following morning we left the building, which was shut up immediately after we had driven out. Nothing was said, but we all shook hands, and the other man gave us both a pat on the back. The young man got in under the back seat, which also had pillows for his head

We set off on the main road to Auschwitz. The snow was frozen and although Sara drove cautiously, we still had one or two slides. After about fifty kilometres, we came to a checkpoint. Sara opened the window and handed the soldier our papers. He checked them thoroughly, saluted, and waved us on our way—so far so good.

We arrived back at Sara's house late afternoon, mainly due to the terrible driving conditions. I got out and opened the garage door, and Sara drove straight in. After shutting the garage door, we lifted the back seat and cover, and the young man got out and stretched, groaning a little.

"Was it very uncomfortable?" I asked him.

"Not at all. Thank you so much for helping us. You are two brave ladies."

We heard a car coming up the drive, and Sara looked out the window.

"It's that confounded Ingrid," she said crossly. The young man was told to go upstairs into a back bedroom, shut the door, and not to come out until one of us went to get him. I opened the door and Ingrid stepped in without an invitation.

"We have only just arrived home after a harrowing journey. What do you want?" I asked rudely.

"I came to let you know that the boys are okay. One of the other officers came home after being slightly injured. I am sorry if I disturbed you."

"I am sorry I was rude. We have been visiting Sara's relative, who actually passed away as soon as we got there, and we are rather tense and tired. Anyway, come in and have a drink, we all need one."

Sara poured three large gin and tonics, and we sat in the sitting room drinking them and making small talk. After we had finished our drinks, we thanked Ingrid for bringing us news of our husbands and both yawned as we showed her to the door.

"We must have a get-together soon," Ingrid said.

"I'll get in touch with you both when I have arranged it. Will you be at your own home, Nicole?"

"Yes, of course. I'll look forward to it," I lied.

"Good night you two, sorry to have disturbed you," Ingrid said as she left.

We left it for ten minutes before going to get the lad.

"Sorry about that. She is a rather noscy person and we are wary of her," Sara explained.

"We will leave it for half an hour, and then Nicole will take you to the church."

By the time we had had something to eat, it was 7:00 p.m. when I left Sara's with the lad. I kept in the shadows and arrived safely at the church.

"I will go and make sure the coast is clear first. Just hide in the bushes until I come for you," I whispered. I went into the church. The vestry door was open, and I found the priest there.

"Is it all right if I bring my companion in?" I asked.

"Of course, Nicole. Please thank Sara for me and that goes for you, too. You are great stalwarts."

I went out of the church and took the lad into the vestry. The priest put his arms round him and, as I took my leave, the lad said, "Thank you so much."

I went my usual secret way home. The house was freezing, so I made a log fire and curled up in front of it wrapped in a blanket. I fell into a deep sleep and dreamed of Sigmund. For some reason when I awoke the following morning I could not fathom where I was. Ridiculous really, but I put it down to the strain of the last few days. I received a short letter from Sigmund that lacked information, which I suppose was obvious, but it was full of love. He told me that he was missing me like crazy and missing our special times—what he called our efforts to rescue as many people as we could. I felt the underlying sadness of what he was doing, knowing how he hated war and the atrocities being carried out at the orders of Hitler and his henchmen.

I decided to go back to my house in Blois, and to this end I wrapped up and made my way to Sara's home. Her welcome was as warm as usual, and as we sat drinking coffee, I told her of my plan to go back to France, where I thought I could do more to help than I could in Auschwitz. Sara was in complete agreement and asked if she could come with me.

"I hoped you would say that. Yes, please come back with me. You will have to bring bed linen as I used most of what I had in some of our missions. The house is tiny, but the Germans occupy the local Chateau at Blois, and naturally there are quite a few traitors to France. I am sure I lost a few friends because of information given by some of the locals. My neighbour Blanche is very nosey, and I don't trust her. A German cook at the Chateau called Eva will, I am sure, help us in any way she can with food and drink, but we must be careful of what we say. I am not completely sure of her loyalty to Hitler. I have no idea how many of the original group of the resistance still exist, but we will find out when we get back."

"I will load the car with all the things we should need. Have you cooking utensils?"

"Not many. I only have a range, and I expect the house has been a 'help-yourself zone' since I married Sigmund."

"Let's get cracking," said Sara standing up raring to get going. I followed her up the stairs where she was pulling blankets, sheets, and other things from her large linen cupboard. These were thrown down the stairs to save effort, followed by pillows and towels. We folded the linens and started packing the car, putting some under the backseat.

"This is going to be a fabulous asset in helping the resistance," Sara said excitedly.

The items collected next came from the kitchen: pots, pans, pottery, and cutlery.

"I think I should take some things from both our houses, perhaps some glasses and decanters, wine from the cellar, and some pictures and ornaments so, outwardly, we can still appear to be living callously and enjoying the confiscated possessions of the Jews."

"That's a brilliant idea, Nicole. I would not have thought of that."

Having put all domestic articles in Sara's car, we then added her best clothes and evening wear in a case and put this with the rest of the luggage in the car. Sara then locked the door and we drove to my home where we picked all the best pieces, a photograph of my wedding in a silver frame and as many bottles of fine wine as was possible to fit in the smallest spaces. I packed my best clothes and evening dresses but also some real tat that we could use in any mission we went on.

"Well, there is no time like the present to set off on our next adventure," Sara said, getting into the car.

We decided that if the priest was not at the church, we would leave a note in the vestry so that if the Polish resistance needed to come our way they would know what to do. However, the priest was there and I gave him the message verbally. He blessed both Sara and I and gave us a big hug.

Chapter 28

On 12 January 1942, Sara and I started out on a hazardous journey to my little house in Blois, France, where we would play the part of wealthy SS officers' wives. We were full of excitement, apprehension, and a little fear, knowing we would entertain high-ranking SS officers who were at the Chateau. We had a long way to go. The snow was patchy with large drifts in some places, icy patches in others, and places with just a few inches until we got nearer to France. The journey through Germany was fraught with danger. We were stopped several times, but again our husbands' names and our papers and passes were sufficient to get us through although the soldiers seemed to delight in holding us up as long as possible. We heard several bombers and blasts as the bombs hit the ground and shook the Earth. We were held up at the border of Germany and France for a considerable time and our documents taken away. We sweated it out while appearing quite calm. When the sentry came back, he smiled at me.

"I'm sorry to have kept you, Frau Lubisch," he said and handed our documents back.

I gave him a cold stare as I imagined a woman of wealth would, and we drove off without a backward glance. We stopped at the first hotel in France we could find, as we were desperately tired and Sara was about to fall asleep at the wheel. It was basic but very clean. The food was homely. They served their own produce and a lovely piece of fish of some sort.

That night there was a bombing raid and our hosts took us to their underground shelter. We spent the rest of the night, fitfully sleeping between aircraft noise, bombs dropping, and their resulting blasts.

"When do you think we will get home?" Sara asked tiredly.

"Probably not until late tonight, I'm afraid," I said and noticed her disappointment.

Once the air raid stopped, we had a few hours of sound sleep. After coffee and some bread, we paid the bill and set off towards Blois.

The rest of our journey was good except for brief stops at two checkpoints, but our papers were checked on the spot and returned. We arrived at my little house just after midnight after a two-day journey, absolutely knackered. We still had to make up beds, a necessity we really needed. My little house was in quite a state. It was dusty and had been ransacked, either by the SS or opportunists. I think poor Sara was dumbfounded when she looked around.

"I'm going to light the range and the sitting room fire to warm the house as much as possible. I suspect that the mattresses will be damp but if we put our raincoats over them and wrap ourselves in blankets we should get a good sleep."

I went into the yard to collect wood, which was covered and quite dry, and soon we had the two fires going. With the range well stocked with dry wood, it quickly heated up the small ground floor, and the small fire in the sitting room eventually got going and sent heat up the stairs.

"Shall we sleep on the floor in front the fire?" asked Sara hopefully.

"Yes, I don't see why not. We have pillows and blankets and the floor is not damp."

We brought some things in from the car but left most things to be brought in the next morning, or later that day to be precise. We had a cup of disgusting coffee and settled down in front of the well-stocked fire and slept fantastically. Neither of us awoke before ten. It was 15 January. We got up and stretched our stiff bodies. Thankfully, we were used to living rough on occasion and soon recovered. We humped in the rest of our luggage, and it filled my little kitchen and sitting room to capacity.

"I told you the house was small." I laughed. "It could be your gatehouse.

I suggest we have a strip wash, put on some finery and makeup, do our hair, and make our way to the Chateau where, hopefully, we will get some provisions and breakfast, if Eva is still there."

"Talking of having a strip wash, my girl, what the hell is that stinking hell hole you call a closet?" Sara said screwing up her face in disgust.

"I kept it like that because I kept my gun and radio behind the panels and hoped the stench would prevent soldiers from searching too thoroughly, which it did on one occasion and saved me from detection."

"Well, that is the first thing we are going to change. When we go to the Chateau, we will ask if they know of someone who will put in a flushing lavatory. That is one step too far for us refined ladies," Sara said in a mock posh voice.

Sigmund

After getting dolled up, not over the top but classy, we walked to the Chateau. Once we arrived, I noticed all the new faces and much tighter security than when I was last there. When we went into the kitchen, I was pleased to find Eva still there.

"Nicole, my dear, how lovely to see you. You look wonderful. Is Sigmund with you?"

"No. He is on the Eastern Front, poor darling."

I introduced Sara to Eva and we then sat around the kitchen table and had delicious coffee and Eva's apple strudel. Bliss!

"Who is in charge here now?" I enquired.

"Obersturmbannführer Anton Bauer. He is pleasant but very pro Hitler, so be careful what you say," Eva said, raising her eyebrows and rolling her eyes.

"We will have to make ourselves known to him. Perhaps you could give him a message that Frau Lubisch and Frau Polinski wish to make his acquaintance."

"Did you say Frau Lubisch?" asked Eva incredulously.

"Yes. We got married in Auschwitz I miss him terribly as does Sara miss Pietre."

"I am so happy for you. You were so in love, it was wonderful to see."

"We better get back home as the house has been empty for a while and there is so much to do. Things are missing, so I think somebody has been in there." We took our leave and as we were going out the door I turned round. "I almost forgot. Do you know of anyone who can put a closet in for us? We only have an outside straw privy, which stinks to high heaven."

"We have some Frenchmen here at the moment doing out Bauer's quarters. I will ask them if they can help."

"Thank you, Eva. The sooner the better!"

"I will take you to a great baker's on the way home," I said to Sara. "He has delicious bread and is a contact. I want him to know I am back."

As we approached the bakery, we saw that several houses in the area had suffered bomb damage and gunfire, probably from executions, but except for bullet-hole scars, the bakery was intact. I hoped the baker was still there. Sara and I went in and the smell of yeast and baking was mouth-watering. There was a young, thin-faced girl behind the counter, and I asked if the baker was there.

"Yes, he is."

"Would you be kind enough to tell him Nicole is here and would like to see him and that she has a very close friend with her that she would like him to meet?" The girl turned and went into the back, and the baker immediately came out, shutting the door behind him.

"Nicole. Thank goodness you are back. We are so short on the ground now. We have lost so many of our group."

"This is Sara Polinski. Both she and I are married to high-ranking German officers and have been doing our bit in Poland and Slovakia. Our husbands are both at the Eastern Front, but they, too, have done good work. I cannot tell you what it is without risking their safety." The baker smiled and gave us some bread.

"Are you still in the same situation at home, Nicole?"

"Yes, and the sooner we get back into the swing of things the better. Sara has a car that has been converted to hide a person, if necessary. However, I am still worried about my neighbour, Blanche. I have not seen her yet, but I have always been wary of her."

We said our farewells and went home where we started to get things in order. The house was nice and warm now with the constant heat from the range. We started on our bedrooms first, hanging expensive pictures, putting out delicate ornaments, and making the beds with Sara's lovely linen and the linen brought from the house that Sigmund and I inhabited whilst in Auschwitz. The lounge was also decorated with beautiful paintings, silver trays containing lovely crystal glasses, decanters, and lovely figurines. Multi-coloured cushions adorned my couch, bringing it to life. Sara had even managed to bring a Persian rug with her, which really made the sitting room quite opulent. We sat down with a cup of good coffee, courtesy of Eva, and admired our handiwork. The fire was alight, and we felt as happy as we could be without our loved ones. We dropped off and were awakened by a knock at the door. I opened it to find a tall German officer standing there with a smile on his face.

"Good evening. My name is Obersturmbannführer Anton Bauer."

"Do come in. It is lovely to see you," I said gushingly.

"This is Frau Polinski, and I am Frau Lubisch. Take a seat, and I will get you some coffee, unless you prefer a glass of wine."

"Actually I would love a glass of wine, red if you have it."

Sara got up, went into the kitchen, and came back with a silver tray on which stood a bottle of good red wine and three lovely crystal glasses. Anton, as he asked us to call him, opened the bottle and poured the wine after having tasted it to check that it was not corked.

"It is very good," he said as he handed Sara and I each a glass.

We sat chatting about the bad weather.

"Nothing like Poland," I told him. "The snow was continuous, and it was freezing cold. I feared that our husbands were suffering atrociously on the Eastern Front. Would it be possible to let our husbands know that we have moved to my house in Blois? It was far too cold in Poland."

"I am sure I can manage to do that for you both. I understand that you need some work carried out."

"Yes, we are without a toilet and only have a straw privy, which is very unhygienic."

"I can arrange that. I have some prisoners working at the Chateau at the moment. They will have to be accompanied by guards, but they could start tomorrow if that is okay. I like to make them work for their lives."

"Thank you, Anton. It is so kind of you," Sara said.

"Well, I don't want to overstay my visit, and will arrange your requests. I would also like you to join me for dinner one night at the Chateau. You know Eva, and she is a great chef."

"We will look forward to that," Sara said. I did not dare speak after his remark about the poor men working for their lives.

When Sara shut the door after him, we both stood there.

Sigmund

"What a dreadful thing to say, and he really meant it," I said. "I could not speak after he said that without making my true feelings known. Well, one of the things we can think about, as there are obviously prisoners at the Chateau, is trying to get some of them away from under the noses of the Germans," I said.

"Great idea. The Germans would be furious and it would be one in the eye for Hitler," Sara answered with enthusiasm. "I think I will have an early night," she said stretching.

"Good idea."

We took turns in the kitchen washing and changing into our warm nightclothes that were hanging on the front of the range and went to bed. I was awakened in the early hours by a hand over my mouth and someone shaking me.

"Can you take someone to the usual rendezvous?"

"I thought that had been compromised," I answered.

"Not anymore," the woman answered. I jumped out of bed and put on my warmest tatty clothes and went to wake Sara. She was already sitting up in bed.

"I have a delivery to make. Do you want to come with me and learn the route?"

"What do you mean, do I want to come? Of course I do." Sara was already donning her oldest clothes.

"We have to be very careful crossing the backyard as I am always worried that Blanche might be watching."

"You lead and I will follow," Sara replied.

The woman went out into the backyard where there was a young Englishman crouched by the hedges at the end of the overgrown garden. We crawled across to him, went through the bushes, and we all rolled down the bank. We crossed the railway line and dashed for the cover of woods. I put my finger to my mouth and beckoned everyone to follow me. I felt exhilarated and frightened at the same time, but I remembered the route. After a half hour, we came across two men. They shook hands with the Englishman and me and left immediately, taking the young woman and the Englishman with them.

I indicated to Sara to crouch down: I put up two hands, touched each finger, and then pointed to my watch. After ten minutes or so, we started to make our way back, deviating slightly. We had no problems getting back and saw no patrols. As we scrambled up the bank, I indicated that we should try to erase, as best we could, any sign of our movements. We crept across the yard and into the kitchen and flopped down on the chairs, feeling mentally exhausted.

"Wow! That was something else," said Sara. "It was really exciting."

"I did not expect anything so soon though," I said. "That's why I leave the doors unlocked always so that they can contact me. They just come and waken me whenever there is a job to be done. I also hide Jews in my cellar."

"Cellar, what cellar?" asked Sara.

"There is a room under the house, accessible only from outside through a skylight hidden behind the fruit crates. Nobody local, other than members of the resistance, knows about it. At times I didn't even know someone was there until they came and told me.

We must have a wash before getting into our beds in case there is a raid. We also must hide our dirty clothes."

The following morning two men, looking poorly and accompanied by a German guard, arrived to build us a toilet. They worked hard and transformed the stinking privy into a toilet with a flushing loo. They whitewashed the walls and obviously had to empty the existing privy in order to demolish it.

"Use your hands," shouted the guard to the workmen.

"It needs cleaning out in the corners and you cannot do that properly with spades."

"No! You will do nothing of the sort. It is a disgusting job in any event, and I will not allow anyone to use their hands to do such a filthy job," I said angrily. The German guard stared at me in amazement.

"As you say, Frau Lubisch, but they are prisoners!"

The men looked relieved, but I did not address them directly again, in case I caused them to suffer more than they already had. They worked very hard and when the guard went out into the street, shackling the prisoners before he went, Sara and I gave them each a glass of milk and bread and cheese. They wolfed it down as quickly as possible, their eyes darting back and forth from the food to the door of the house.

"Don't worry, I will intercept the guard if he comes back into the house. There is no back entrance," Sara reassured them in Polish, to their amazement.

It was quite a while before the guard returned. He had been conversing with Blanche, and I wondered what she had been gossiping about. The glasses and plates had been taken away and washed, leaving no sign of food.

"Would you like a coffee?" Sara asked the guard sweetly in perfect German.

"Yes, madam, I would be very grateful for a drink. I am parched."

"You probably have been talking too much," I could not help saying. He looked at me strangely. I must try to curb my tongue before I give myself away.

The workers left at six that evening after having laboured hard.

"They will be back tomorrow to finish off, however long it takes. Lazy sods," the guard said as they went out into the street.

I held my tongue and just smiled weakly at them. Sara and I looked at each other.

"You must try not to retaliate when the Germans make comments, Nicole. Otherwise, you will fall under suspicion."

"I know. I just can't stop myself, but I will try hard to keep my mouth shut."

We lit the sitting room fire, poured ourselves a glass of wine, and sat there contemplating the previous night.

"How often does this happen, Nicole?"

"It can happen several nights on the trot or weeks can pass," I answered.

We had some pâté on lovely fresh bread that Sara had gotten from the bakers when she walked into town to see if there was any news. The next couple of days passed quickly. The men finished the toilet, nothing fancy but so much better than the privy, and a sergeant from Bauer's office came with an invitation to join him for dinner, the evening of 20 January. This was a couple of days away and we were excited that we might hear news of Sigmund and Pietre and even some war gossip as, of course, we were Germans!

The next two days passed uneventfully and on the morning of the twentieth, we started pampering ourselves. We gave each other manicures and pedicures. After washing it out thoroughly, we lugged the bath in, so we could each have a leisurely bathe. Sara gave me some beautiful body cream, which I applied liberally. We washed our hair and, when it was dry, brushed it until it shone. Sara told me to add camomile to the water when rinsing my hair, and it really did make a difference. When I walked, my hair was bouncy and my loose curls wispy. I decided to wear it down for this evening's appointment. Sara was going to let her black hair hang loose, and it framed her fair-skinned face beautifully.

All this pampering took up much of the day, mainly because it took so long to heat the water for our baths. In no time at all, we were applying our makeup with extra care and donning our gowns. I chose to wear my understated but sexy green-silk dress that Sigmund loved so much. Sara chose a midnight-blue, classic-style dress, which went with her blue eyes. To be absolutely vain, we both looked like a million dollars.

A car arrived at 7:15 p.m. to take us to the Chateau, where quite a number of guests were mingling together in the great entrance hall. When we entered, we caused quite a stir, especially amongst the men. We were announced formally as Frau Sigmund Lubisch and Frau Pietre Polinski, and then by our Christian names, Nicole and Sara.

We were served copious amount of wonderful Champagne and eventually summoned to the dining room for dinner. Of course, Sara and I were separated and placed next to unattached males. I was seated next to a handsome young man, Kristopher Klimens, and Sara was next to Hans Gruberg, a very high-ranking Nazi, Gestapo actually. We all had happy and light-hearted conversations whilst being served a lovely dinner, again courtesy of Eva. After dinner, we all went into the large sitting room, one I had not seen before.

"Have you heard from your husband, Nicole?" Kristopher asked with obvious interest. "I have heard that we are having difficulty holding our own and have sustained massive casualties."

"I haven't heard much, just a short, non-committal note, but I gathered from the tone of his words that it was very hard. I think he prefers it to being posted at Auschwitz." I said this before I realised what I was saying, me and my big mouth.

"I utterly agree with his sentiments, Nicole, as do several guests here tonight, but we all have to appear loyal to the *führer*. There are many ears listening for dissent amongst the ranks and some are here tonight."

"I think we should change the subject. Would you mind getting me another glass of that delicious red wine?"

"It will be my pleasure, Nicole," said the charming Kristopher. At that point Sara and Hans Gruberg joined us.

"Hello, you two. Are you enjoying yourselves?" Sara asked cheerily, slightly slurring her words.

"I'm just going to get Nicole a glass of wine. Can I bring you one, too?"

"I think not. I have had far too much already. I think Hans here has been trying to get me inebriated. I would love a coffee though," Sara said looking at me and raising her eyes to the ceiling. She was obviously bored stiff with her dinner partner.

"Sit here, Sara. This is a spare chair." Sara immediately sat down and Hans wandered off in the direction of the bar.

"My, what a bore and definitely a fan of Hitler, so watch what you say," Sara warned.

Kristopher came back with my wine and told Sara that her coffee would be coming shortly.

"Thank you."

"This is Kristopher," I said to her. "I don't think you have been introduced properly."

"No, we haven't. My name is Kristopher, and I am glad to meet a friend of this charming, young lady. I know your name is Sara because Nicole has been singing your praises most of the evening. What are you both doing in Blois?"

"My parents have a little house here and we both wanted to get out of Poland. It was freezing cold there, and we were unable to get enough supplies, so when Sigmund and Pietre went to the Eastern Front, we thought we would come here to stay. It is much warmer and produce is easier to come by," I explained. "I also found the fact that thousands of Jews and other ethnic minorities were being exterminated in the same town hard to bear." I saw Sara glare at me crossly.

"I also cannot believe what is happening in these camps and to the prisoners of war." Kristopher was most sincere and solemn when he said this, and I thought that it would be nice to introduce him to Sigmund when he was home on leave.

"What do you do here at the Chateau, Kristopher?" asked Sara.

"I was badly wounded last year and spent nearly a year in hospital. I had to have a lung removed and my spleen, so I am confined to a desk job now. All very boring."

Sara looked at her watch. "It's after 1:00 a.m., Nicole. I think we should make a move."

"Yes. I did not realise it was so late. I have really enjoyed the evening and your company, Kristopher."

"The same applies to me, Nicole. I hope we all meet again." His smile was directed at Sara as well as me.

When we reached the entrance to the Chateau, a staff car was waiting to take us home. In the car, we carried on a normal conversation about how pleasant the evening was and talked about the good company we were with. However, once we were home, Sara nearly exploded.

"What a horrible man that Hans is. He is definitely in favour of executing the Jews and is a great fan of Hitler, Himmler, and Goering, amongst others." Sara poured a large measure of whisky and held out the glass to me, which I declined.

"I think I will stick to wine, thanks anyway." My eyes looked round the room, and I realised that there was something different. "I think we may have visitors in the cellar, Sara, or we are going on a mission. The furniture has been moved, one of our covert signs." As I finished speaking, there was a loud banging on the door. I opened it to find two soldiers standing there and a truck containing others parked in the road.

"Can I help you?" I enquired coolly although my heart was thumping in my chest.

"Your neighbour has reported some activity on your premises. Can we come in and look round, Frau Lubisch?"

"Of course. I can assure you that there is only Frau Polinski and myself on these premises. We have just spent the evening with Obersturmbannführer Anton Bauer at the Chateau."

"We must insist that we check, Frau Lubisch. These are our orders from Obersturmbannführer Bauer, and they must be obeyed. He must be concerned for your safety."

Sara and I sat in our chairs sipping our drinks whilst the two soldiers stomped all over my little house. They then went out into the backyard and had a good search around there too.

"Well, it seems that it was a false alarm, but we cannot let anything happen to two of our most admired senior officers' wives. We will leave you in peace, but don't worry about anything as we will be patrolling the area for the rest of the night."

As I shut the door, I had to lean back on it, such was the tension that I had been under whilst they were searching my house.

"That bloody woman, she has been trying to cause trouble since I came here to live and especially since I met Sigmund. She calls me a German whore, the bitch." I was absolutely fuming once I overcame my fear of anyone being detected in the cellar. I knocked back my wine just as the air raid warning sounded.

"Here they come. God bless them. Perhaps they will make a direct hit on the Chateau, but I think they are trying to wipe out the submarine base at La Rochelle. We have nowhere to hide, so we might as well go to bed and keep our fingers crossed."

"What if there are people in the cellar?" Sara asked.

"We can't do anything about them. Whoever brought them will come and get them when arrangements are made for their onward transit. We must, however, let the baker know that Blanche has reported activities on my premises and that she will be watching like a hawk at all hours now."

The sky lit up and several enormous explosions occurred in the direction of the coast. Even as faraway as they were, their impact made my little house shake—Sara and me too! We both hoped that if we had guests in the cellar, they were not too terrified. The all clear did not sound until morning, and there were several smaller explosions nearby from bombers dropping their spare bombs in hopes of hitting strategic areas on their way home to England.

The following morning Sara went to the bakers to let him know that Blanche had reported the comings and goings at my house and if there were people in my cellar, they must be removed as soon as possible. Sara suggested that if we knew when the resistance was going to remove the visitors in my cellar, we could invite Blanche and, possibly, Bauer, Kristian, and Hans to dinner. We could ply them with lots of wine and generally make as much noise as we could whilst those in the cellar were being removed.

The baker was most concerned and said they would be removed as soon as possible and thought our idea was a sensible one. He also mentioned that Blanche had been suspected for quite a while in causing the deaths of some resistance members.

Chapter 29

Sara collected a delicious loaf and a potato pie for the party.

"I think that Blanche will be bumped off soon. In fact, I could do it myself!" I said, thinking of Claude and all the other brave men who had been caught and executed.

We looked at the lovely pieces of furniture and ornaments purloined from Jewish homes that had been taken over by the Nazis. We had made this little house into a rather luxurious home and looked forward to showing it off to Blanche, who would be green with envy. The rest of the day Sara and I went for a long walk, taking in possible hiding places should the need arise.

We visited the baker, who asked us to arrange the dinner party for the coming Friday, 26 January, and when we eventually arrived home, I realised I would have to blag some provision from Eva. Bauer had already arranged for us to receive sufficient provisions for us to live quite comfortably, but Sara and I wanted to really show off. Eva, as usual, promised to help with fish, cheese, coffee, butter, and some tin pâté. We could put on quite a spread with these ingredients together with eggs, bread, and potato pie from the baker who wanted the evening to be successful for obvious reasons.

Sara was the one to invite Blanche, and she accepted immediately, probably because she was dying to see inside my house and meet up with high-ranking German officers. We had no call to go out on a mission, and I think the main aim was to get whoever was in the cellar away safely. This frustrated me in that I was doing nothing to help those who needed to escape Nazi cruelty.

We had no news of our loved ones apart from hearing that all was not well on the Eastern Front with vast numbers of casualties. On our last visit to the Chateau, Bauer boasted about the treasures that Nazis were stealing from the opulent Russian palaces, virtually stripping some of them bare. Of course, Hitler and his close cronies requisitioned the loot. No doubt some minor officers got their share as well.

Sara and I were busy all day Friday cooking and making the house shine. Sara made a lovely apple tart glazed with some precious brown sugar from Eva. We decided that we would really doll ourselves up, mainly to annoy Blanche and to show off some of the fine jewellery that had been given to our husbands after it was stolen from the Jews. We would make it one of our priorities at the end of the war to return it to the Jewish government since it would be impossible to return it to its rightful owners. In the meantime, we had given the baker an expensive piece of jewellery to help with the cost of getting prisoners to safety, whatever their race.

Anton Bauer was the first to arrive, accompanied by Kristofer and the awful Hans. Eva had declined our invitation, but a French woman, rather attractive and a collaborator, accompanied Bauer. Blanche arrived shortly after, and her eyes nearly fell out of their sockets when she saw our home and the luxurious things we had in it. Her eyes then took in the jewels that Sara and I were adorned with that matched our expensive gowns. Mine, borrowed from Sara, brought out my fine complexion, and Blanche was unable to hide her jealousy.

We served our guests the finest Champagne in the thinnest crystal glasses followed by copious amounts of the best wine, courtesy of the rich pickings we all had from living in the homes of wealthy Jews. My heart gave a twinge at the thought of their demise or imprisonment, but we had to keep up our pretence or all our efforts to save as many as we could or sabotage as much as possible would be to no avail. We had lovely titbits that Sara had made: some lovely stuffed wild mushrooms, and, of course, a beautiful potato pie, a gift from the baker. The evening went without a hitch. Nobody wanted to use the loo, which had been our biggest worry. We laughed and flirted and, all in all, the evening was a great success.

At 1:30 a.m. Anton said he must take his leave as he was going on manoeuvres that morning for a couple of weeks. Kristofer joined him, as did Hans and the French woman who thanked us profusely for a lovely evening. A staff car arrived as if by magic, apparently prearranged to be at my address at one-thirty on the dot. We waved them off and shut the door, forgetting that Blanche was still in the house.

"Well, I must say you have done well for yourselves fraternising with the Nazis."

"I am married to a Nazi, Blanche, and I did not hear you complain about your company tonight," I said heatedly. Blanche went to the door and had a last sarcastic look round and left.

"Bloody bitch. I could easily be the one to shoot her," Sara said menacingly.

We left the tidying up until morning and did not rise until ten. I was still in my robe when there was a knock at the door. It was Anton on his way to manoeuvres as several trucks of soldiers were lined up behind his car.

"Nicole, I have some bad news for you I'm afraid. Sigmund has been badly injured and is in a field hospital somewhere in Germany. I don't know any other details, but I left instructions at the Chateau to let you know if more news comes through. I am very sorry, but I thought you should know."

"Thank you, Anton," I calmly answered and as he turned to get into his car. I shut the door and then clung to the chair in front of me.

"At least he is alive, Nicole. You must not give up," said Sara, putting her arms around me. "We must try to get a mission to occupy ourselves as soon as possible," she continued whilst putting the coffee on. "We will have breakfast and then go see the baker, the sooner we get ourselves occupied the better."

We dressed and had a leisurely walk to the bakers. When we got there, the shop was mobbed. He had received a delivery of flour and had baked bread. Rather than wait, we went back into the street and wandered up to the Chateau to see Eva. It was not our lucky day; Eva was not there, and her replacement did not know when she would be back. We strolled around and saw quite a lot of damage south of town where the bombs had been dropped too early on the raids of La Rochelle. We returned to the bakers and found the shop empty of both people and bread. The baker came from the back with a small loaf in his hand for us.

"You are so kind, thank you. My husband has been injured on the Eastern Front, and we need a mission to occupy ourselves and help all we can."

"I will contact the resistance. I know that their numbers have been depleted after a few were caught last week. By the way, your visitors got to their contacts safely."

"Thank goodness. We were terrified that someone would want to go to the loo whilst they were getting them out of the cellar."

The baker then said that he was sure we could be used in a mission that was going to occur near Niort and told us we would be contacted.

"Something needs to be done about Blanche. I am sure she is reporting whatever she finds out to someone."

"That, too, is going to be sorted out," the baker said, opening the door for us to leave. He did not like us hanging around too long.

Chapter 30

As we leisurely strolled home, two German soldiers recognised us and waved; we returned the compliment. Once back home we set to, clearing up the mess from the previous evening. We had not been working long when there was a knock at the door, and a young man dressed in the postal delivery garb of the French stood there.

"I have an urgent message for Frau Lubisch." My heart sank as I thought the worst.

"Thank you," said Sara taking the envelope from the young man who winked as he turned away and cycled off on his bicycle.

"He was not from the post office," Sara said happily.

We tore open the envelope excitedly and found instructions for us to help in the sabotage of a committee room in the Castle at Niort, a beautiful medieval castle on the banks of the Sèvre Niortaise River. It was renowned for its deep dungeons where it was suspected that some prisoners were being kept and tortured. Apparently several top members of the SS were going to hold a vital meeting there to discuss the strategic moves on the Eastern Front, which was undergoing devastating losses and injuries.

Our job was to carry out a diversion by setting off a small bomb to the south of the castle. We were instructed where and when we could find the bomb and when to explode it. We would have no personal contact with any of the other participants of the mission, and we were instructed to burn the instructions immediately after reading them. Enclosed in the envelope was a message notifying me that Sigmund had been injured, not a genuine document but was very plausible to anyone looking at it.

We were to do our bit at precisely eight o'clock the following Tuesday evening, 1 February. This would entail hiding out in position for the better part of the day to avoid being seen breaking curfew. We did not go to Niort to sus out the position in case we drew attention to ourselves, but we knew we would be guided to our position if necessary. We were certain, however, we could find it. I had previous knowledge of the area around the castle from when I was sending radio messages.

The weekend went by and we were both a little bored, although excited about our latest mission. On Monday, we went to the bakers to see if he had any bread or message for us. Unfortunately he had neither, but he did have a few potato scones that looked appetizing enough. We bought these and he wished us luck as we left the shop.

Tuesday, 1 February was a grey dismal day, cold with occasional showers of sleet and heavy snowflakes. We were dressed as warmly as possible and looked as though we had both put on weight. As I stood by my bedroom window, I saw Blanche go out.

"Sara, I think we should go. Blanche has gone out, and she will not be able to see us go through the back hedge."

"Okay, I am ready. I have the scones in my pocket so we won't starve."

We left the house unlocked as usual and made our way down the bank and into the woods. We had a long way to go on foot. It was amazing how I remembered the tracts. We had frequent breaks to listen for patrols and heard a bombing raid going on far in the distance, which was probably beneficial to us since it was occupying most of the German troops in the area. We traipsed on, slipping and sliding on the wet and snow-covered tracts, hardly daring to speak to each other in case we were heard.

We reached the south of Niort at about four that afternoon and it was already dark. We went down to the river's edge and took a precarious route to our allotted position. Once there, we made ourselves as invisible as we could and remained completely silent waiting for our contact. The contact happened to be a young woman, probably no more than eighteen. Although we did not speak, we all shook hands, and she adeptly demonstrated how to set off the homemade bomb. We checked that our watches were set to the same time, and she left as silently as she had arrived.

We sat hidden from view for the next couple of hours. At two minutes to eight, Sara took the bomb and primed it. She moved away to what we had been told was a safe distance, at all times watching the second hand on her watch. As soon as it clicked to eight, she exploded the bomb. The noise was deafening, and when the smoke subsided, I saw Sara lying on the ground covered in blood. I crawled as quickly as I could over to where she lay and dragged her away from the site of the explosion. Luckily, she was unconscious and could feel no pain.

I dragged her as fast as I could, probably causing more damage. I felt a hand on my shoulder and turned to see a young man. He picked Sara up and beckoned for me to follow him. As he did so, there was a loud explosion from within the castle at Niort. I followed him, trying to help as best I could. It was obvious that Sara was dead weight for him to carry. We ended up in a damp, dark cave with a single candle burning towards the back. When we got to the back, there was a table, apparently used to patch up wounded resistance members. There were one or two camp beds, one already occupied by somebody seriously injured or ill. Two men took Sara and laid her gently on the table and began to remove her clothes.

"It's all right. We are medics," the elder of the two said. Sara started to moan. Her face, her hands, and parts of her legs were black.

"I am afraid she has some burns to her face, hands, and legs. Unfortunately, her legs have been partly skinned from dragging her away from the scene, but that of course was a necessity. Most of the burns are not too bad, but some may scar her permanently."

The two medics started working on her whilst I sat in the gloom and cried. The young man gave me a glass of brandy and told me to drink it down, which I did.

"Where's Nicole?" I heard Sara say. "Is she all right?"

"I'm here. I am not hurt at all."

The medics worked gently and confidently on Sara's wounds, and I went over to her and let her see me. Her poor face looked completely raw. Sara tried to smile, but her face was taut and looked very painful.

"I think someone put too much explosive in the bomb," Sara said.

"I am so sorry," said the young man who had carried her. "I made the bomb."

"I have to tell you that the mission was successful and several senior SS officers were either killed or injured. God help all the local people as there will be a price to pay for our success." The elder man told us, sounding delighted with the outcome. It seemed a callous attitude, but it was the success of defeating the Nazis that was upmost in everybody's minds.

One of the medics said confidently, "Now that we have cleaned your face, the skin does not seem to be deeply injured. The wounds are just superficial and once the rawness has gone, there will be no scars on your face. Your legs, however, will probably have some scarring."

"How are we going to explain Sara's injuries?" I asked the people around us.

"I think the best thing to do is light a paraffin lamp and drop it so it leaves some burns on your carpet and on some clothes that you have removed. Get Nicole to throw water all over you after you have removed the clothes and the floor is burnt, then Nicole should shout for help. The most difficult thing is to get you home without being seen. It is going to be painful, but it is better than being caught as a spy," said the man who was leader of this resistance cell. "Thank you both. You have been brave in the extreme and have been a constant source in our fight against the Nazis. We owe you a great debt, but I think you must give up any activities for a while."

Getting Sara home was indeed difficult. Sometimes she was carried and sometimes she had to crawl along the ground, causing her more pain. It took hours getting back because we had to lie low until dark. Eventually, we climbed up the bank and into my house. The men left immediately.

I lit a paraffin lamp as directed, and Sara took off her clothes and dropped them haphazardly on the floor, so it looked as though she had torn them off and dropped them where she was standing. I dropped the lamp as hard as I could and it exploded into flames, immediately catching the linoleum flooring in the kitchen and Sara's clothes. I threw a large basin of water over Sara causing her to scream. I opened the front door and screamed for help. Luckily, two sentries were checking that the curfew was not being broken, and both knew who we were. They dashed to our aid and threw more water on the burning floor.

"I will go and get a doctor," one of them said. "I will be as quick as I can," he said and set off at a hell of a pace. The second soldier and I draped a cotton sheet round Sara, and it seemed no time at all before the local doctor was pushed through the front door. The soldiers waited outside whilst the doctor examined Sara.

"I think you have been very lucky. One would think that you had already been treated."

"Don't be ridiculous," Sara said. "It only just happened. Nicole dropped that lit paraffin lamp on the floor. The only treatment I have had is Nicole throwing a bucket of extremely cold water over me."

"As it happens, that was the best thing she could have done. You should continue to bathe your face in cold water. Your legs need to be dressed in places, but I think they will heal without leaving too much scarring."

He dressed the wounds and said he would be back in the morning to see how Sara was. He acted suspicious, but I thought it best not to mention this to Sara. We thanked the soldiers and I started to clean up. The smell from the burnt linoleum was toxic, so I opened all the windows and doors even though it was freezing outside. There was a lot of glass around so I had to be ultra careful. I knew Sara was in pain, but her face had already begun to lose some of its redness, thanks to whatever treatment the resistant medics gave her.

"Well, that was indeed some adventure," Sara said with a wry smile.

"We did what they wanted us to do, but it is dreadful that you were hurt," I answered. "I am sure we can get a German doctor if you would like. I bet one will come anyway after the soldiers reach the Chateau and tell them what has happened."

Sure enough, an hour later Dr Herman Gruger called. He checked Sara over and said that apart from her legs there should be no permanent scarring. "It looks like you have been professionally treated already," Dr Gruger said as he packed his bag.

"Only by freezing cold water," Sara said calmly. Dr Gruger looked at us both and asked if we had heard how our husbands were doing.

"Unfortunately, Sigmund is in a field hospital somewhere in Germany, but as far as we know Pietre is still okay and on the Eastern Front. It would be wonderful if we could hear from them. We miss them terribly," I said, tears welling in my eyes.

"I will try to find out how they are, but I can't promise I will be successful. There is such fierce fighting on the Eastern

Front. We should draw back, but Hitler is adamant that we achieve victory over the Soviets, it seems at any cost," said Dr Gruger, openly disagreeing with Hitler's tactics.

It seems that Hitler's hatred of the Soviets is deep-seated and nearly as bad as his hatred of the Jews. I wondered at that point how the few we managed to help escape were faring and thought about Sigmund's bravery in getting them out of the camp. It was so few, but at least we achieved something. We offered Dr Gruger a glass of wine and when he accepted, we decided to join him.

When he left, I suggested to Sara that I go to the Chateau to see if they had any spare flooring for the kitchen and when Sara said she was going to nap, I did just that. The wind was biting but I was well wrapped up. Eva was in the kitchen of the Chateau and I asked her if there was a housekeeper as I needed some linoleum. "Yes we have a new housekeeper but beware she is another Eva Braun (a euphemism for a hard hearted and sour faced woman). I don't trust her one jot." answered Eva

Eva poured me a coffee and, of course, treated me to her apple strudel, which seemed in endless supply. She left the room and was gone for quite a while but returned with a sour faced, typical Nazi woman.

"Eva says you are scrounging for some flooring." No introduction was forthcoming, so I did not introduce myself either, although Eva must have told her who I was. "I have a large piece of linoleum that you can have. It is a rather a sickly shade of green, but it will cover your damaged floor. I will get the workmen to bring it. Of course, soldiers will accompany them. Make sure they do the job properly."

With that last remark, she left the room. Eva raised her eyebrows but did not comment. She did not seem her usual happy-go-lucky self, but I did not question her about it. Obviously there were changes at the Chateau.

"You must come and visit us, Eva. It would be a nice change for you and no doubt you would bring a strudel," I said tongue-in-check.

"Actually, I would like that, Nicole. I would like to see Sara too, poor thing."

Just then the air raid siren went, and I shot off as fast as I could. When I returned home, Sara was still asleep. I made coffee, courtesy of Eva, and awakened her with a large chunk of strudel and coffee.

"Wow! Eva's back," Sara said.

"Yes, but she does not seem her usual self. There is a hard-faced Nazi as a housekeeper, and I think this is one of the reasons. Also, there are changes at the Chateau, not all good I suspect. However, I managed to get some lino, and the housekeeper is sending two men to lay it, of course accompanied by soldiers. They are probably the same men who did the privy."

I checked Sara's legs, which were badly blistered, and she had a nasty skinless patch on the side of her right check, which looked as though it could scar. I did not tell Sara about my concerns but just smiled at her and asked if she felt okay. The sirens went off again, but the bombing sounded as if it were in the vicinity of La Rochelle. We remained safe.

The following morning, 3 February 1942, the two emaciated Jewish men turned up with their military escorts and wasted no time pulling up the burnt lino. I kept the soldiers occupied, chatting to them as Sara gave the men a glass of milk containing a raw egg. Sounds pretty awful, but at least it would give them a little nourishment. The prisoners worked hard and did an excellent job, but it still took most of the day to replace the lino. It was just the colour that was awful.

At lunchtime I made coffee, and we had cheese and fresh bread that Sara made. I managed to sneak some bread and cheese to the workmen who ate it as quickly as possible, obviously terrified they would be caught. Sara and I flirted with the soldiers and, acting like typical men, they lapped it up and paid no heed to their wards. After I tidied up and put the biggest rug we had over the lino, we sat quietly with our own thoughts.

"I feel wasted just sitting here and not helping the war effort. I might visit the baker tomorrow."

"Please be careful, Nicole. I think some of the Nazis are beginning to have doubts about us," Sara said worriedly.

"Thousands of innocent people are dying because of Hitler's hatred of the Jews, Soviets, and other ethnic minorities. I can't just sit here. Perhaps I could volunteer as a nurse at one of the German field hospitals. There must be people there who need help, and I might even come across Sigmund. It would cheer him up immensely if he did not see me and I put my hand under his covers and gave him a familiar grope."

I laughed at this but the seed was planted in my mind, and I would enquire at the Chateau about helping in one of the Nazi field hospitals in Germany. I was pretty up-to-date with first aid and could pretty much bluff my way through most things. We retired to our rooms and slept well. I dreamed a delicious dream of Sigmund making love to me in his special way and I must have had a smile on my face whilst I slept.

Chapter 31

The following morning was dank and cold, but I wrapped up and set off for the Chateau to volunteer as a nurse at the field hospitals. It was 4 September 1942, and once again I would be starting on another adventure. Obersturmbannführer Anton Bauer was there and seemed genuinely pleased to see me.

"Hi, Nicole. How is Sara after your fire?"

"Not too bad. The blisters on her legs are quite bad and some of these will leave scarring, but her face should heal completely." I did not mention the patch of skin that concerned me on Sara's face. "I will come straight to the point and tell you my reason for calling on you without warning. I was wondering if you need any nurses for the field hospitals in Germany. I have basic nursing training and I am a quick learner. I feel I must do something for the war effort whilst Sigmund is lying wounded in some field hospital."

"I can tell you without hesitation, Nicole, that we are desperate for nurses. I don't know where you would be sent, but I think probably within Germany. I will contact Obersturmbannführer Schneider, who is a doctor and recruits as well. I should get an answer pretty quickly. How soon can you go?"

"Immediately if necessary," I answered. "I won't keep you, Anton. You must be very busy. I will get my bits and pieces together, hopefully in preparation for my new career in nursing."

"It won't be pleasant, Nicole. The injuries are sometimes horrendous, and the conditions at the hospitals are basic. They are short of most things. I am sure, though, if anyone can cope you can."

We said our farewells and Anton asked me to give his best to Sara. When I arrived home, Sara told me Dr Gruger had visited her while I was at the Chateau, and was delighted with her progress.

"I might even be able to join you, Nicole, in a few weeks."

"That would be great, and I am sure the baker will probably find you something to do in the meantime. The cellar might be used again in extreme emergencies, and someone has to keep an eye on Blanche, perhaps even knock her off," I said laughingly.

I was extremely excited about my possible new role and hoped that I would hear soon as to my posting or training. Sara was happy for me, but we would miss each other dearly as we had become as close as family.

It was three days later, 7 February 1942, when a messenger from Anton told me that I should enrol in the DAK (German Red Cross) where I would receive a refresher course and then be sent to a *feldlazarett* (field hospital) more than likely on the Eastern Front where casualties were high. Anton had made arrangements for me to meet Dr Schneider on 10 February, when he would be attending a dinner at the Chateau. He would arrange for me to join the Medical Corps via the DAK. Anton also asked if Sara and I would like to join them for cocktails at eight. This would be after the meal since the dinner was arranged as a strategic meeting and civilians would not be invited to attend any such meeting. We told the messenger that we would be delighted to attend for cocktails.

Sara and I lazed around rather a lot over the next few days, but on the tenth we spent the day titivating ourselves. Sara's face was much better and showed hardly any sign of the effects of the blast, but her legs were quite blistered and still needed dressing. Luckily, we were going to wear long gowns.

As usual, Anton sent a car for us, and when we arrived at the Chateau the meeting was over. All the participants were in the lounge enjoying the lovely wines from the Chateau's cellar, and Anton immediately introduced us to Dr Schneider, a sharp-faced, middle-aged man who seemed to look down his nose when speaking. Sara looked at me and pulled a face, and I found it hard not to laugh. Sara was certainly getting back to her old self.

Kristopher was there and about twelve other officers, most of whom asked after Sigmund and Pietre but whose names we could not remember. No one, it seemed, had any news about where Sigmund was but confirmed that Pietre was still on the Eastern Front. After a few drinks Dr Schneider came over to me.

"I understand you wish to help out in our *feldlazaretts* and that you have basic nursing training."

"Yes, I would like to do something useful for the war effort, and I understand that you are very short of nurses."

"Sadly, that is the case," he answered solemnly. "If you feel ready, I could arrange for you to be taken to the Ost. Front where we have many casualties. I am afraid it will not be pleasant and there are many risks. If you should be captured by the Russians, it would be certain death in the most barbaric way."

I thought to myself that they were just getting their own back for the millions of people and prisoners that they have starved and are still starving to death.

"I can go at any time, Dr Schneider. I am a woman of leisure," I replied glibly.

"I will be in touch very shortly. There is a DAK convoy leaving soon, and I think they will be able to take you. Anyway, I must be on my way. Thank you for volunteering." He clicked his heels and went to say his farewells to Anton and the larger group of officers.

I turned to Sara. "What a pompous ass. I didn't dare look at you in case we both burst out laughing. Can you look down your nose when you speak?" This was the final straw, and we collapsed in hysterical laughter.

Anton came over. "Can I share the joke?" he asked smiling.

"I don't think you would be amused," Sara said, still giggling.

"You never know, we might have the same thoughts. I assume the joke was at Dr Schneider's expense."

"Well you will never know, Anton. You will just have to keep guessing," Sara said, fluttering her eyelids.

Anton walked away laughing. Shortly after this, a car was summoned and we went home where we fell into our comfortable chairs and laughed at nothing, really; we were just in that kind of mood.

"Let's have a drink," I said. "I feel like getting blotto."

"Me too," my friend replied and got a bottle of wine and two glasses.

We made short work of this, so we had another bottle. We just could not stop laughing, the wine adding to our uncontrollable mirth. The next morning two very dishevelled specimens came down into the kitchen with the inevitable hangovers.

"I will make the coffee," I said, my head thudding every time I moved. "I think I may have my coffee and then lie down for a bit."

"I will join you. I have a hell of a hangover but can't complain—it is self-inflicted. I won't say never again, because we'll do it again."

"Too true," I said as I put my coffee on the side table and collapsed into the chair. We spent the rest of the day feeling sorry for ourselves and had an early night. The next day, 12 February, we both got up wide-eyed and pain free.

"I thought we could have a stroll to the bakers just to let him know what I am going to do."

"I want him to know that I will be available for minor missions until I am able to join you," Sara said. "I am going to feel very lonely without you. I might see if I can get a job in the Chateau where I might glean some useful information to pass on to the resistance."

When we got to the bakery it was closed, and there was no sign of life. We walked round the building to no avail. As we were leaving, a young man came out of a nearby house and started to do something to his windows.

As we passed and without turning towards us, he said, "The baker was arrested last night. I don't know any details, but I would advise you not to come here again. Another contact will be allotted to you and make themselves known when it is safe to do so."

We continued walking as though nothing had happened and went straight to the Chateau to see if we could find out anything. Eva was alone in the kitchen, and the hatchet-faced housekeeper was nowhere to be seen.

"Where is the housekeeper?" I asked.

"Most likely watching any torture that is going on," Eva said bitterly. "She is a cruel woman who has been sent to help weed out resistance members. There are a couple of them here at the moment going through hell, I should imagine."

Eva became tight-lipped after this, and we just chatted about mundane things until the air raid warning went off.

"Come on, girls, we must get down to the cellars," said Eva in a bit of a panic.

We followed her via a different route than normal. I suspect that the prisoners were in a part of the cellar that they did not want us to be near. The planes must have been flying quite low as the antiaircraft guns were going at it nineteen to the dozen. There was a large explosion that shook the Chateau, whether this was a downed plane or a bomb we did not know. Whilst we were in the cellar, Anton came in.

"I thought I caught a glimpse of you two coming up the drive. I think that you best settle down for the night as our intelligence says this is going to be a long raid."

"Thanks, Anton. I was wondering if I could be of some help here in the Chateau whilst Nicole is away. I don't mind what I do, within limits of course," said Sara.

"Actually, I don't think Nicole is going to be faraway. Dr Schneider has assigned her to the Wehrmacht troop *feldlazarett* at Aubeterre sur Dronne which is near Poitier," Anton informed us.

"Oh. That's great. I will be able to come home when I have leave if indeed I get any leave," I said brightly.

We had another glass of wine—we never learn—and then settled down for the night on camp beds that were not too bad. We slept well, although I thought I heard someone scream during the night but could not be certain, and I did not want to seem nosey. In the morning we rinsed our faces and then went up to the kitchen for breakfast. Anton joined us together with Kristofer and both wished me good luck in my new role as a nurse.

"I can't believe I am going to be close to home," I said. "Did you have anything to do with it, Anton?"

"Maybe—maybe not," he said, smiling. "I think you will be going tomorrow, 14 February. Be here at eight. A troop carrier will take you on their way to Poitier."

"Okay, I will be here ready and willing to work my socks off, and hopefully I will find out something about Sigmund."

Sara and I decided that we would walk home and declined the offer of being driven. We said our good-byes and went out into a lovely bright morning, although with frost still on the ground it was cold.

"Did you hear someone screaming last night?" I asked Sara.

"Yes. I have a terrible feeling that the baker is in that cellar somewhere. There is a chance that he may give us away if he is unable to tolerate the pain and atrocities that he will certainly suffer at the hands of the Gestapo."

"We will just have to brazen it out. I think even the Gestapo would find it hard to believe that wives of two high-ranking officers would be involved in espionage. We can also blame Blanche for making untrue accusations."

I tried to act light hearted, but I was concerned that we might be questioned. If I left tomorrow, Sara would be alone here, and I would probably be questioned at the field hospital at Auberterre sur Dronne.

Chapter 32

I set off early the next morning for the *feldlazarett* and arrived fairly quickly as it was not very far, a mere fifty miles or so. When I arrived, I was appalled at the conditions at the hospital. The wounded had no more cover than tarpaulins stretched over a framework with the sides open to the elements. It was cold, muddy, and filthy. The moans of the wounded were heartrending even though they were mainly Germans. Their dressings were filthy, and their attire filthy, bloody, and vomit stained; there was an overwhelming stench of urine and faeces.

I was introduced to the senior doctor, Dr Becker, who was young and seemed to be at his wits end. There were three other nurses all hard-faced and probably SS. I asked how many patients there were. They did not know, because the dead had not been counted that morning although they estimated ninety-two.

"There is one English pig of an officer here too, but the doctor insists we treat him in accordance with the Geneva Convention," said Sylvie, the largest and most butch of the nurses—a most inappropriate name I thought.

I asked if there was any spare linen that was not suitable for bed coverings, which could be used as dressings. There was a filthy pile of bloody dressings laying in a pile on the floor.

"Why the hell are these rags laying here? Have you not been taught anything about infection?"

This was greeted by stony looks and no answer. I picked up the rags in two goes, lit a fire, and collected a couple of buckets of water to boil. Once the water was boiling fiercely, I put in the rags sparingly, so they would have a chance for sterilisation. Dr Becker came over and thanked me.

"You don't have to thank me, it is my job as a nurse to help the wounded as much as I can. By the way, my name is Frau Nicole Lubisch. My husband Obersturmbannführer Lubisch was serving on the Eastern Front and was wounded, and he is now in a field hospital somewhere in Germany."

"I am so relieved that I have somebody with some decency to help me. Those other three are sadistic to say the least, especially to the English officer who is severely wounded. I am sure I will have to carry out amputation on him if I cannot get the infections in his wounds under control."

"I can speak English if that is of help to you. I also speak French as well as my native German," I lied. "We must collect as many plants with antibacterial properties as we can—like garlic, peppermint, calendula, roses, and St John's Wart—to make poultices and lotions, and creams. They will be better than nothing, as I assume you are short of everything."

"God. I am so glad you are here, Nicole—may I call you *Nicole?*"

"Of course. We must get those nurses scrubbing every surface, spare camp beds, and utensils. That should put a smile on their faces." I laughed.

Once all the rags had finished boiling, they looked much better and were at least clean. I hung them on an improvised line and with the strong wind they should be dry in no time. Dr Becker put the nurses to scrubbing all clear surfaces and the spare beds with carbolic soap while he scrubbed and scrubbed the operating table. He seemed to be filled with a new sense of purpose. I suggested that we start going round to the prisoners, renewing their dressings as soon as the rags were dry. I found clean clothes for some and put redlined tags on those who were too ill to recover. I asked Dr Becker if he had been in touch with headquarters to ask for drugs, linens, and other supplies, and he said that he had not received a reply. I asked if he had a car and he did.

"Can I borrow it? I am going back to the Chateau to get whatever I can and will be gone a few hours. These soldiers cannot be left to lie in their own squalor. Can you take me to see the English prisoner, so I can see what can be done for him?"

"Certainly. His name is Major Sinclair. He is in pretty bad shape." The smell was obnoxious when we went into the area occupied by Major Sinclair.

"Hello. My name is Nicole Lubisch. I am a new nurse stationed at the field hospital. I apologise for the appalling conditions, but all here are in the same boat. We will do our best to improve things. Is there anything you want?"

"Please, could I have a wash and some clean clothes? I stink. I could do with something for the pain, too, it is getting unbearable."

Dr Becker said he would get something to ease his pain but explained that he had no strong analgesics at the moment. After we left Major Sinclair, I went straight to Dr Becker's car and drove as fast as I could to the Chateau at Blois. I went straight in the back and found Eva and the housekeeper in the kitchen.

"What can I do for you, Frau Lubisch?" the housekeeper asked coldly.

"I need linen, towels, pyjamas, and any other male attire that is available. I am at the field hospital at Auberterre sur Donne, and the soldiers are in a terrible state. The young doctor has hardly any medicine or anything else to give those poor souls comfort. I need soap as well and bottles of spirit that we can use as antiseptic."

Much to my surprise the housekeeper asked Eva and I to follow her. We went to a linen cupboard stacked with sheets, towels, pillows, and pillowcases.

"Take as much as you can," the housekeeper said, addressing both Eva and myself. "I will go and get blankets and bring them to your car. Pyjamas will be a bit of a problem, but I am sure we can find some and also long johns that will suffice with vests."

"Thank you so much. You can't imagine the squalor those poor boys are lying in, and most of them have infections. Quite a few are awaiting amputations and some are dying."

By now the car was jammed packed with all the aforementioned items as well as other things: disinfectant, painkillers, clothes pegs, washing powder, and bleach. Eva had made up a cardboard box of essentials such as dried milk, dried eggs, sugar, coffee, and salt. I thanked them profusely, asked them to let Sara know I had been there, and set off back to the hospital with a laden car.

When I arrived back at Auberterre sur Donne, the doctor's and nurses' eyes nearly popped out of their heads, but we lost no time in washing the patients with soap and putting them in clean clothes. We then put sheets and a blanket on most of the beds. I must admit that the nurses had done a good job with the scrubbing, and the whole place looked respectable and smelt so much better. Unfortunately, two patients had died of their wounds, and the allocated prisoners of war were digging their graves. They were so malnourished that their arms looked as if they would break with each shovel full of earth they dug. This was something I intended to change. Prisoners of war needed to be fed in order to be able to carry out manual work.

I explained my plan to Dr Becker, and he actually agreed that the prisoners should be fed larger amounts of bread and given milk. I thought to myself that this was better than the scraps that the poor men were able to beg for or the leftover food that came from the patients' plates. Obviously these scraps were contaminated by those with infections. I got him to agree to give them apples, which were in abundance after having been harvested and packed last autumn at the surrounding orchards.

I went to change Major Sinclair's dressings and found him in a sorry state. The smell emanating from the wound in his left leg was worrying, and I was pretty certain he had gangrene in it. When I took off his filthy dressings, my concern was realised: it definitely had gangrened. I rapidly went to get Dr Becker, who showed no surprise whatsoever, much to my chagrin.

"Aren't you going to amputate his lower limb, Dr Becker? You cannot in all humanity let the poor man rot to death, even if he is the enemy."

"Frau Lubisch, I will operate on him when I see fit. I am the doctor here."

I walked away from him muttering *bastard* under my breath. It was unusual for Dr Becker to be short with me, so I put it down to exhaustion. However, the next day he actually amputated Major Sinclair's leg. Major Sinclair was a great stoic. He was not given nearly enough analgesics, so I tried to slip him some tablets when I was alone with him and saw no one was outside the ward.

The problem of cleanliness was so much better now that beds were changed frequently and linens boiled. Dressings were replaced regularly, and the general running of the hospital was much more efficient.

A week later, February 21, I decided to visit Sara to find out if she had news of the baker. When I got to the house, she was still there but just about to leave for the Chateau where she had an administrative post.

"Have you found out anything about the baker?" were my first words to Sara.

"Oh, Nicole, he has been shot. It was him we heard screaming, but he gave no one away. Even Kristofer said he was one of the bravest men he had come across."

"Poor man. We will have to find out who will be our contact. There is an English Major at the hospital who has had his leg amputated, but once he is on the mend, we must get him out of there. He is being neglected and would have literally rotted away if I had not spoken to Dr Becker, who was not pleased and would certainly not have operated on the him had I not intervened."

"My God, Nicole, just how are we going to get him out of the field hospital?" Sara asked incredulously.

"With God's help, and luck. Once he is well enough, I can get him out of the tented area where he is, and we can arrange for someone to be there to drag him away. There is no side to his tent, so he will be able to roll himself out in the direction advised by his rescuers. I can cause a diversion by creating an emergency. In any event, there are so few people working there I think it should be quite easy. I will have to leave you to find help, Sara. Many men are being brought to the hospital daily, so I am unable to leave often. I wish I could find someone who knows where Sigmund is."

"I don't want to rub salt in your wounds, but I heard from Pietre. He thinks he should get some leave soon. Whether he can come here, I don't know, but if not I will meet him in Poland or Germany."

"That's wonderful news, Sara. Have you any idea when that will be?"

"Next month he thinks, around the twentieth of March. He seems quite upbeat, but they are taking very heavy casualties. At least it is getting slightly warmer and is no longer below freezing."

Chapter 33

Another exciting and perhaps dangerous mission to get the major to safety was foremost in my mind, and I knew Sara would do her level best to try to contact the resistance. Easier said than done with so many of them having been executed.

I worked my socks off at the hospital everyday. One day merged into another and before I knew it, it was time for Sara to see Pietre. There were so many young men, boys really, with horrific injuries and so few staff that we were usually always nearly dead on our feet by the time we had our breaks. A lad called Frederick asked me tearfully if I would hold his hand one evening, which I did without hesitation.

He looked at me with watery blue eyes, tears streaming down his face, and asked, "Will you let my mother know I died bravely?"

"Of course I will," I replied, squeezing his hand.

He was only sixteen when he died two hours later, and even though he was the enemy, I wept. All those in the hospital were conscripts, and I could hardly feel ill will toward any of them.

I really wanted to see Sara before she went to meet Pietre, to find about the arrangements if any, to move Major Sinclair who was making remarkable progress and hopping round his bed and to the loo. I will have to speak to him soon about moving him out before he is sent to a prisoner of war camp. Amazingly, Sara turned up to see me, laden with surgical provisions for the patients and a crate of potatoes from the cellars. Eva had sent several strudels, so the patients and I had a nice treat.

"I am going to Poland to see Pietre and stay in our house there, he thinks for about a month, and we will try to find out where Sigmund is. I am off later today but have found you a friend. You will have to go to the village church where someone will meet you. They think it's possible to help the major and will make him crutches, but he won't be allowed to have them here, in case he can use them to escape."

We laughed at this remark and embraced while, at the same time, kissing each other on both cheeks. Sara left quickly because we were becoming emotional and this was no way for two strong, brave women to behave.

It was a fine day with blue skies, a few clouds, and a March wind, which made it quite cold. After I finished changing the dressings of those who were under my care and putting the bandages on to boil, I asked Dr Becker if he would mind my going to the village church to pray for the safe return of my husband.

"Nicole, of course you can. You have worked tirelessly for weeks and have never moaned or feigned illness like some of your colleagues. Say a prayer for me too, please."

I put on my warm cape and a large scarf over my nurse's uniform and made my way to the village, where the Nazis occupied a few small terraced cottages and, of course, a large house with a well-tended garden. The church was small and very neglected. There was a hole in the roof and the plaster was falling off the walls. I knelt in a pew, bowed my head, and said a prayer for Sigmund and even Dr Becker. I sat back and looked at the young girl in the pew in front of me.

"Are you Nicole?" she asked.

"Yes, but you should not ask the names of people you have been sent to contact. I might have been an enemy stooge."

"I am so sorry, but I have no time. We want you to get the major outside the north side of the tent later on when it's dark, at 1:00 a.m." The girl then got up and left. How on Earth was I going to arrange this immediately?

I managed to tell Major Sinclair what had been arranged, and he said he could easily get himself out of bed and out of the tented area where he was being held. He thanked me, but I said that it was the resistance he should thank for taking untold risks daily, many of whom had been executed. I gave him some painkillers to take whilst he was being transported to where he would be hidden.

That night was mayhem. Many severely wounded soldiers were brought in, two of which were dying. We worked so hard.

Later, Dr Becker came into the ward. "I think you should get some rest, Nicole, it is already 2:30 a.m., and we have a full list of surgeries ahead of us tomorrow, nothing too bad by our standards but bad enough."

"Thank you, I will. I am almost out on my feet, mainly emotional tiredness from being with those two lads, their poor families. Good night, Dr Becker."

"Good night, Nicole, sleep sound."

I could not believe the time, but I dared not check to see if the major had gone. I was lying on my bunk fully clothed and fell immediately into a deep sleep. The next morning one of the nurses had to wake me. I had slept so soundly, I did not hear the commotion going on.

"The major's gone," the nurse said incredulously. "How on Earth does a man with only one leg escape? They have sent out a search party from the local barracks, but there is no sign of anything untoward in his tent."

"Say that again, please, and say it slowly. I am only half awake," I said as if butter would not melt in my mouth.

"The major has gone," the nurse reiterated, "sometime during the night."

"I can hardly believe it. A man with an amputated leg that is barely healed has escaped."

"Yes, that's right. The doctor thinks that Special Forces must be in the area as he could not manage alone."

"I don't know. Desperation can cause enough adrenaline for someone like that to escape, but I don't think he will get far," I said, hoping that this would not prove to be true.

I washed my face in cold water to stay awake. I had slept in my clothes and didn't have to dress, so I went into the treatment area where I found Dr Becker.

"How on Earth did that man get away in the condition he was in?" I asked.

"I have no idea. Someone must have helped him. The question is who? If Special Forces were in the area, some kind of action would have been taken on their part, like blowing up the ammunition store. I think it must have been the resistance."

"Is there any resistance left in the area? I thought most had been executed."

"I thought so too, but they are a very resilient force, I must say; you have to admire their bravery."

I was most surprised to hear Dr Becker, someone dedicated to the *führer*, say this.

Our conversation was short-lived, as several soldiers with dreadful injuries were brought into the treatment area. Two had the red-rimmed tags tied to their wrists, so they were placed outside the treatment area where a nurse would sit with them until they passed away. Neither was conscious, thank goodness.

Dr Becker operated on those who required surgery, helped by Dr Leichner, a woman doctor who had arrived yesterday. We all worked tirelessly until the early hours of the following morning, all thoughts of Major Sinclair gone from our minds. When all the patients had been treated, we checked the wounds and dressings of the other patients. Whilst doing this I fainted. When I awoke, I was in bed wearing a clean nightgown after apparently having had a bed bath. I knew because I smelt so much fresher than I had the day before. Dr Leichner came to see me and said that I was utterly exhausted and should go home for a complete rest and that I was not going to be of help in the state that I was in.

"Have you not been eating proper?" she asked. "You are so thin. I would say that you are nearly emaciated."

"I actually don't know if I have been eating properly. I seem to have been working nonstop," I told her and started to cry.

"We must get you home as soon as we can, and you must have complete rest and nourishment and no worries. I think you are clinically depressed and missing your husband desperately, with the extra strain of not knowing where he is." She put her arms around me and hugged me.

"I want you to take this. It will calm you, and I will make arrangements for you to be taken to your home. Eva from the Chateau is arranging for food to be put in your house that I am sure you will enjoy. She will also check on you until your friend comes back from seeing her husband."

True to her word, Dr Leichner arranged for a car to take me back to my home in Blois. This was a rather hairy journey because a daytime raid was taking place around La Rochelle. Bombs were being dropped not far from our route. My luck was with me once again, and I arrived unscathed at my little home, now feeling like a luxury, where I found Eva. When she put her arms around me, I once again burst into tears.

"Come on, Nicole, let's get you to bed. No arguments. I will bring you a hot drink and a piece of your favourite apple strudel, and then you can sleep for as long as you can and start to recuperate. You are so thin and weary looking, Sigmund would not recognise you."

Eva bustled around getting my nightclothes and nearly lifting me physically into my bed. This was bliss, my lovely bed with my linens. She propped me up on vast feather pillows while I drank hot chocolate and ate apple strudel.

"I will be off now and leave you in peace but will be back later with a nourishing meal for you."

"Thank you, Eva, you are so kind."

I finished my drink and strudel and cuddled up in my bed; in no time at all, I fell fast asleep. I did not wake until dark, and I could hear a noise downstairs and heard the bath being filled.

"Come on, my sweet. I have run you a lovely bath scented with lavender, and I will wash your hair for you. Supper will be served after your bath, some lovely broth full of goodness, and a small steak and vegetables followed by a light mousse. I am sure you will enjoy it."

I luxuriated in the bath and allowed Eva to wash my hair and dry and brush it. I felt so pampered and already felt so much better. Both Eva and I enjoyed a delicious meal with some lovely wine to wash it down. We sat chatting for a while, and Eva asked if I had found out where Sigmund was and was disappointed that I did not know anything.

"You must get really well, Nicole, and not think of going back to the hospital for at least a month. Sara should be back by then to keep you in check."

Sara was, in fact, coming home around about 9 April, and I looked forward to her return. I had missed her not being around. I soon returned to my old self and in no time it was time for Eva to return home. I had definitely put on weight and my hair was back to its shiny best. Eva had just left after bringing my evening meal, and I was sitting reading a book when the front door opened and Sigmund stood there.

I was dumbfounded and all I could think of saying was, "Darling, why did you not let me know you were coming home."

"I wanted to surprise you, my dearest, dearest wife. I have been longing to see you, aching for you, and now I am actually here."

We rushed into each other arms, our bodies pressed as close together as they could get. In no time we were kissing passionately, our hands touching each other in our intimate places, and without further ado, we were both naked and making love on the floor.

"Stop, Sigmund, it is about to happen to me, and I want it to last as long as possible."

We lay still for a very short while, but our resolve was weak and we ended up with a body-draining climax at the same time. We both said "I love you" at the same time and then looked at each other. Sigmund had scars down the front of his chest and quite significant burn scars round his neck and upper part of his back.

"Oh darling, was it awful. Did you suffer a lot?"

"Nowhere near what the others suffered. You don't find my scars off-putting, darling, do you?"

"Don't be ridiculous. I love you with all my heart and nothing can stop me wanting you every time I see you, speaking of which, shall we go upstairs?"

Not another word was spoken for quite some time as our touching each other again excited us to the height of passion and beyond. As we lay back exhausted, we asked each other what had happened since we last saw each other. Sigmund had been through hell and back and had lost many of his men. I told him of my work in the field hospital, the escape of Major Sinclair and that Sara and I were still in touch and helping the rather depleted resistance movement.

We fell asleep in each other's arms and slept like babies until a very surprised and excited Eva arrived with breakfast. Eva lost no time in telling Sigmund that I had been so physically and mentally exhausted that I was sent home from the field hospital. Eva dished up homemade muesli full of nuts, dried fruits, and bran, enough to feed three or four people. A large glass of creamy milk was also placed in front of me, and Eva stood guard whilst I ate as much as I could.

"That's my girl," said Sigmund as I put down my spoon and pushed myself away from the table, feeling full and quite uncomfortable.

"It's your turn now, Sigmund, isn't it, Eva?"

"It certainly is, although he does not look as if he has been short of nourishment."

Sigmund laughed and started eating a much smaller amount of muesli but just as large a glass of the delicious, creamy milk. "There you are, it's like being at school again," Sigmund said as he took his last mouthful.

"Well, how are you, Eva? Thank you for looking after the love of my life."

"It was a pleasure, Sigmund, and I am quite well, thank you."

After Eva had left to return to the Chateau, we decided that we would have a sexy bath time, soaping each other tenderly and touching each other in our erotic places. When we finished our bath, we lay on the towels and made love.

"We were definitely made for each other," Sigmund said adoringly, as I lay naked on the floor.

I noticed the effect I was having on him so I sat up and said, "Oh no, my darling, not again. Try to wait until bedtime, if possible, and I will do the same. We have so much to catch up on. First of all, when will you have to go back on active service and where will you go?"

"I am going to be spared fighting on the front and may even be posted to the Chateau again, if I'm lucky."

Sigmund

"Oh, my darling, that would be wonderful, and we will be able to carry out some missions."

"Nicole, we must be extremely vigilant. Everyone is on tenterhooks because of the continual bombing of submarine bases, especially as we have and are still losing so many men on the Eastern Front. Hitler will not hear of our moving back. His hatred of the Russians is without bounds. The soldiers being sent there now are just youths."

"I am always very careful. Sara and I had a bit of a scare when they arrested the baker, but he did not succumb to the dreadful torture he had to endure, and we were all safe. The only thing now is that I do not know who is on my side and won't know until Sara gets back."

"How are we going to manage when Sara gets back? The house is lovely but not big enough for three."

"I thought you could move out to the barracks," I said laughingly.

Sigmund grabbed me. "Then I had better make hay while the sun shines."

"No you don't. You're sex mad. I reckon you have been taking pills to increase your libido."

Now I was in for it. Sigmund dragged me to him, threw me over his shoulder, and carried me upstairs, where he threw me on the bed and, with no finesse whatsoever, made love to me in every position imaginable.

"There you are, you minx, I knew we wouldn't make it through the day without having sex."

"You cheated and overpowered me," I said, a smile beaming all over my flushed face.

Our days were spent together in bliss for the next week. Sigmund had heard that he was to be deployed at the Chateau and would be allocated married quarters there, which solved the problem of the house. Sara would be quite happy to be on her own and, of course, would be welcome anytime to our new home. Sara was due back tomorrow, 9 April, and would be really surprised and pleased to see Sigmund.

That afternoon Sigmund and I walked up to the Chateau to view our quarters. We were delighted to find that our first floor apartment was beautifully furnished and faced the gorgeous grounds.

"It's really lovely, and I am looking forward to moving in," I said rather distractedly.

"What are you thinking about?" Sigmund asked.

"I was wondering what sort of work you would be doing."

"Trust you to start planning as soon as you get wind of my impending employment here. I think you might be pleasantly surprised!"

Sigmund smiled broadly when he said this, but I knew better than to question him further whilst we were in the Chateau. We went down to see Eva and had coffee with her and a piece of a sponge cake, which was nearly as good as her strudel. Eva was pleased to hear that Sara would be back the next day and asked if we needed provisions for her.

"Actually, we still have quite a good larder at the moment. Sara can get what she wants after she arrives, but thanks, Eva, you have been so kind to us."

The new housekeeper walked in and introduced herself to Sigmund, hardly able to take her eyes of him. I actually felt a pang of jealously. "I understand you are taking over one of our apartments whilst you work here Obersturmbannführer Lubisch. I hope you will both be comfortable, but please let me know if there is anything I can do to make your stay a pleasant one. When will you be moving in?"

"We would like to move in tomorrow evening when Frau Polinski returns from visiting her husband and takes over my house in the village."

"That will be fine. The apartment has already been thoroughly cleaned and there is everything in the apartment to meet your needs, I am sure." With that the housekeeper left the kitchen.

We finished our coffees, said our good-byes to Eva, and left for home with an invitation to join her for dinner with Sara. It seemed strange that I would be returning to the Chateau again when Sara and I could carry out a mission. Hopefully, Sigmund would be able to give me information that could help the allies. I would have to try arrange to use a radio once Sara was back and felt quite excited that I could once again get one over on the Nazis. I think Sigmund looked forward to helping me with my efforts to help the allies, to assuage his guilt at the cruelty metered out by the Germans.

Sara arrived safely the following day looking well and affluent as usual and was absolutely delighted to see Sigmund. She gave us news of Pietre and said that according to him, it was horrendous on the Eastern Front. She said that he looked drawn but was generally fit physically; however, he was struggling mentally.

"Sigmund and I are going to move into the Chateau where he will be working mainly on logistics, but hopefully he can give us some information to pass on. Do you know if there is a radio available so that we can pass anything useful to the allies? I would like to have it in my care and would be happy to send messages for the resistance."

"Yes, I have made contact with a woman, and we rendezvous in the caves outside of Niort. I had a couple of visitors in the cellar whilst you were away but didn't know who they were or their nationality. Their arrival and removal were carried out without a hitch."

"Are you up to coming to the Chateau with us for a meal prepared by Eva? She is looking forward to seeing you."

"Yes, I am very hungry, and I don't feel like eating alone either."

"We thought it best if you had the cottage to yourself. It is too small for the three of us, and I will have an excuse to leave the Chateau to visit you by car, and we can then meet up with whoever can let me use a radio. I need to get in touch with my headquarters. I have not radioed in a considerable time. Of course, you are most welcome to come to our apartment as often as you like."

We all had a wonderful dinner with Eva and Anton Bauer, who was anxious to get news of Pietre and discuss Sigmund's post with him. As usual, we had lots of the lovely wine from the cellars. Following the meal, Anton and Sigmund went to Anton's study whilst the three of us were left with the wine.

Chapter 34

Sara was taken home by staff car, and I said I would visit with her the following day to liaise on our future missions. It was yet another chapter in our lives, and I really needed to let headquarters know of the terrible happenings at Auschwitz and find out if the people we had rescued made it to safety. I would tell them that Sara and I were still alive and ready for whatever action came our way. I was desperate for Sigmund to find something useful for me to transmit.

We went to our apartment and, for once, just lay in each other's arms without any thought of making love. Sigmund's wounds had healed very well but, of course, the burns scars would never go away.

"Do you start in the office tomorrow, darling?" I asked.

"Is tomorrow the eleventh?" Sigmund asked sleepily.

"No, it's the tenth."

"Well, that is the starting date of my office job." No sooner had he said this than he began his usual soft purring, rather than snoring, and I followed suit shortly after.

The next morning after Sigmund had gone to the office, I dressed in some of my best clothes, put on some striking jewellery, asked for the staff car that I had been allocated, and drove down to Sara. She, too, was dressed to kill. We set off in the direction of Niort and parked the car in the small square near the castle. We window-shopped virtually empty windows, went into a café full of SS officers for coffee, and lingered over our drinks. At one-thirty we walked along the river until we came to what used to be a beautiful park but was now overgrown and filled with rubble from the bombings. Nobody was about so we went towards the cave entrance.

When we went inside, a gentleman's voice told us the radio was where it was originally, on the other side of the bridge in Niort and down the same track. He said there were numerous soldiers around, but they did not appear to be seeking anything in particular. We turned round and walked slowly back to our car. Several SS officers passed us and nodded, and we returned the courtesy with a "good afternoon." We both felt very smug knowing that we were going to get one over on them again, hopefully.

We drove sedately over the bridge and kept going along the road, missing as many potholes as we could. When we came to the track that I had used initially, I stopped the car, got out my compact, and checked my makeup and the surrounding areas with my mirror.

"Do you want to come with me, or would you rather stay in the car?"

"I am coming with you. You can teach me to send messages at the same time you are messaging."

After ten minutes or so we came across the radio's hiding place, and I lost no time contacting my controller in England who was pleased all was well with me. I told him of the atrocities being carried out in Auschwitz and in the concentration camp in Bergen-Belson, near the town of Cella, which was a camp where the Nazis were starving thousands of men, women, and children. He informed me that the allies were beginning to gain momentum and the RAF lads were doing wonderful work but taking heavy losses. I asked him to let my parents know I was well but not to mention I was married.

Sara was amazed at how quickly I sent and received messages. I took the radio and walked in a completely different direction before hiding it in a pile of rubble. We then took a different route back to the main road and our car. As we approached the car, a truck carrying soldiers stopped.

"What are you doing?" the driver asked.

"We are having a walk and a comfort break," I said trying to act embarrassed.

"I am Frau Polinski and this is Frau Lubisch from the Chateau at Blois," said Sara haughtily.

"Sorry to trouble you, Frau Polinski. I served under your husband at Auschwitz when he was a doctor there." Sara made no comment but just got in the car and powdered her nose.

"Will you dine with us tonight, Sara? I think Sigmund has arranged for one or two other officers to come—Anton, Frederick, and I am not sure who the others are, but I suspect they are all of like minds regarding Hitler."

"That would be nice. Perhaps we can persuade them to have a go at Hitler."

"We will do nothing of the sort. They may be loyal to the *führer* for all we know and Sigmund would be labelled as a traitor."

"It was a tongue-in-cheek remark, Nicole. I am not that dumb."

We stopped in the marketplace at Blois and went for a coffee hoping that somebody would see us and have a message or consignment, but this was not the case, so we went back to the Chateau and made ourselves a couple of martinis.

The evening was very pleasant indeed, even Eva came, and there was a distinct air of disillusionment towards Hitler and the dreadful atrocities being carried out. Nobody suggested assassination though, much to mine and Sara's disappointment. As usual, we had one too many drinks, so Sara stayed the night. In the morning after a night of several air raids, we decided, against Sigmund's, advice to take a walk.

"There will be plenty of places to hide if there is another air raid," Sara told Sigmund, who looked at us both sternly.

"I know what you are trying to do and I fear for you. Whenever you go out, I feel sick with worry."

"Don't worry, my dearest, we are invincible." I said smiling.

"If only that were true," Sigmund said, hugging me to him. He knew all too well that we would be looking for some way to help someone in peril.

However, the next evening Sigmund came home with news that the Nazis were trying out a long-range rocket, more than capable of reaching England. This news was just what we had been dreading.

"You will not do anything about this tonight. I will drive you and Sara where your radio is tomorrow evening and you can send your message then. Kristofer lives with his companion in the other side of Niort and if we are stopped and questioned, which I doubt, I will say we are either going to or coming from his home where we had been for drinks. I will mention this to my colleagues during the day."

I was beside myself with excitement and could hardly sleep a wink. As soon as Sigmund had left in the morning, I dashed to see Sara to tell her the news.

"Isn't Sigmund putting himself unnecessarily at risk by taking us?" Sara asked worriedly.

"Yes, I am sure he is, but he insists that he is going at any cost. He just wants to make amends in any way he can for the atrocities carried out by his countrymen."

"What time will we be going, do you think?"

"I expect about 6:30 p.m. As soon as he has washed and changed, we will pick you up. Cocktail dresses I think will be the best thing for us to wear. I just hope the radio is still there. I think we should go and have a coffee in the square again in case we are able to contact any resistance members to let them know we wish to use the radio. They will surely know if it still in situ."

We wandered into the square at Blois but were unable to make contact with the resistance. We then went into the church, but no one was there either. We lit two candles and left to go to our respective homes until it was time to meet for our next mission.

Sigmund came home early, and we dressed as if we were going to a party. Then we went to pick up Sara. She had also dressed in suitable attire for a cocktail party, and we set off for Niort in high spirits. We drove over the bridge at Niort, and I started looking out for the track I had to go down. A first I missed it because there was more rubble caused by heavy raids. Sigmund turned the car, and we drove back slowly until

I recognised the area where the track was or had been. Sara and I got out and clambered over the rubble, and we must have looked comical dressed as we were. Sigmund stayed in the car with the engine running. We had decided on the excuse that we had to make a comfort stop because of eating something that was off. We walked and clambered all over the area where I knew I had hidden the radio but without success. We checked thoroughly again to no avail before making our way back to the car.

"It is not there, Sigmund. Do you think the SS found it?"

"I am pretty sure that I would have heard about it if they had. When we get back to our apartment, I will see if there is a radio that you can use. It is going to be very risky as the majority of my colleagues are very jumpy at the moment, but it is an absolute necessity to inform your handler so that the RAF can reconnoitre near the French coast and farther to see if they can find the launching sites. The problem is that the launching equipment is mobile and can be moved quite easily."

"I would prefer it if you went home, Sara, so that if anything goes wrong you will still be around to carry on our work," I said apprehensively.

"I actually agree with you although I feel like a coward because I won't be with you when you send the message, but I know our work must go on," Sara replied.

We dropped Sara at my house and drove back to the Chateau where we entered laughing and cuddling each other on our way to our apartment, acting as though we had actually been to a party. Once inside, Sigmund said that he was going to find a radio and bring it to our apartment.

"Get ready for bed, and I will bring the radio to you and also get into bed. You can send the message, and we will keep the radio in bed with us. If there is any sign of disturbance, we can pretend to be in the throes of lovemaking. We should also have some wine so that our breath smells of alcohol."

"You would make a wonderful spy, my darling, but please be ultra careful."

"I will, and please put on a really sexy nightdress as we may, hopefully, not have to pretend."

Sigmund's eyes were twinkling at the thought of making love. Although we had calmed down in our passion, we still enjoyed a wonderful sex life that seemed to get better and better. After Sigmund left to find a radio, I decided that the sexiest night attire would be nothing at all, bar a dab of expensive perfume between my breasts.

Sigmund was gone for nearly half an hour. When he came back, he entered the room furtively carrying a bulky blanket. He came straight over to the bed and looked at me admiringly, but because of the importance of our mission, he kept his hands to himself. He sat on the bed, unwrapped the radio from the blanket, and handed it to me. I immediately sent the message as concisely as I could, signed off, and put the radio between us in the bed, pushing it farther down the bed. We cuddled together full of tension while waiting for a ruckus to erupt. In fact, nothing happened, but we were both too pent up to make love and slept fitfully.

In the morning we carried on as normally as we could, had breakfast, and Sigmund left for his office. I got out a large shopping bag, put the radio in, and topped it up with clothing and a few knick-knacks. I dressed smartly and made myself up immaculately before setting off for Sara's. As soon as I was in sight of the house, Sara came out of the door, obviously wanting me to hurry.

Chapter 35

"We did it Sara. We did it," I said excitedly.

"How did Sigmund get the radio?" Sara asked.

"I actually don't know, but it is here in my bag, and we must find a new hiding place for it so we can use it when necessary. Have you any ideas?"

"How about in the range? I do not use it, and if it is cold, I can light the fires in the living room and bedroom."

"It is not ideal, but since I have no other suggestions, that is what we will do. Perhaps we can make a false bottom in the oven so that it looks as though it is empty, similar to what is under the seat in your car, but much smaller of course."

"I think that is the only option until we make contact with someone from the resistance," Sara said thoughtfully.

"I don't know how we can do it, but we should start experimenting straight away. Have you seen any large pieces of wood about the size of the inside of the oven that we can paint black?"

"No, but there is a piece of metal sheeting left from the conversion of the privy, but we will have to bend it to shape as we have no way to cut it. It is pretty rusty and would do well without painting, as some parts of the inside of the oven are rusty."

"Let's have a go, Sara. We will have to do it inside in case there are prying eyes," I said. "I'm pretty sure my father had a hammer somewhere. I'll see if I can find it." I started looking in the boxes in the kitchen that had not yet been opened.

"There is one in my car boot," Sara said.

"Good for you, Sara, you always seem to come up trumps," I said, hugging her tightly.

We got on with the task at hand and, although I say it myself, we made a pretty good job of it. Once we had stowed the radio we put the false oven base in. Heaven help us, a pretty botched job if anyone searched thoroughly. We decided to go to the church and then to the café in case there was anyone linked to the resistance. It was a lovely April day, quite warm, as May was only a few days away. The church looked pretty with the flowers that grew up each year coming into bloom. When we went inside, the priest came out of the vestry and nodded to us. We lit a candle, and as we did so the priest came over to us.

"Are you Nicole?" he asked, and I nodded.

"As you see I am new to the area and don't know the names of my parishioners, but I have been told of you and understand that both you and your friend have done some wonderful work for the War effort."

Neither of us answered him. It was well known that some priests had betrayed members of the resistance to save their own skin.

"Would you care to join me for a glass of wine?" he asked.

"That would be very pleasant. Thank you," Sara answered immediately, and we followed him into the vestry. He went to the window and placed a vase on the windowsill.

"Would you prefer red or white?" he enquired, getting a bottle of each out of the cupboard.

"Red, please, for both of us," Sara told him.

We sat and drank our wine and answered his questions regarding our husbands and how we were coping with the lack of food. We did not admit that we were well supplied at the Chateau. Sometime later the outside door opened and a middle-aged, haggard, and frail-looking man came in. He looked Sara and I up and down and then came over to us and took our hands.

"Thank you for all the help you have given us. My name is Charles, and I am a member of the resistance. Are you still willing to help us?" Sara and I looked at each other, both wary of giving ourselves away to a collaborator. "I knew Claude, Pierre, and the others. Fortunately, we found the traitor and he has been dealt with. I also know that you shot Maurice as he, too, was a traitor."

I was the first to speak. "You look as if you could do with a hearty meal."

"Yes, as do many people round here."

"I will get you some provisions. I am afraid it will not be much, but it will certainly help. We will deliver some here tonight before the curfew." With that we left.

"Do you think they are genuine, Sara?"

"Yes, I do," Sara said emphatically. "I am absolutely certain."

"Well, we better get some provision to them. Have you got much to spare? I will go back to the Chateau and see what I can glean without the housekeeper's knowledge. I will meet you at the church at 5:00 p.m."

We went our separate ways, got all that we could, and met back at the church as arranged. Charles was already there, and his eyes nearly popped when we placed the provisions on the vestry table.

"I am afraid this is a one-off Charles. The housekeeper at the Chateau is strict and a supporter of Hitler's regime, and I am very wary of her. She probably checks what each individual takes."

"This is fantastic and will be shared out equally to those in need. Thank you so much. If you are able to help us, we will leave messages of what is required at the vestry."

Sara and I took our leave and went to our respective homes. When Sigmund came to the apartment after work, he said that a radio was missing and a thorough search of the Chateau was taking place.

"Well, they won't find anything here," I said smugly.

"I think Frederick is suspicious of us, but I am not too worried. I know, if it was possible, he would do the same, but it is something that we must not speak of."

There were continual air raids going on all around our region, but Blois was luckily hardly ever hit. The news from the Eastern Front was bad. The Russians were holding out against all odds, and the Germans were still taking heavy losses, but Hitler was determined to wipe out the Russians come hell or high water regardless of the cost to his men, just boys really. Another attempt had been made to assassinate Hitler but was unsuccessful again, and the officers concerned had been executed. The allies were doing better since America joined the war but were still sustaining heave loses as they battled to regain France. The RAF and the USAF were bombing strategic positions in Germany and lookout planes were apparently looking for possible German rocket-launching sites.

Sigmund put his arms round me and began to nuzzle the back of my neck, his hands creeping slowly and sensually towards my breasts. Even at the beginning of Sigmund's foreplay, I began to feel hot and my juices were flowing. I placed my hands on his hardness, and he caught his breath as he turned me round and kissed me with such tenderness I felt like crying.

"I love you so much, Nicole, so much it hurts."

"You know I feel the same, Sigmund, and I want you to make gentle and long-lasting love to me." This was a certainty, and we did not even bother to get up following our lovemaking, as we had fortuitously taken a bottle of wine with us when we first went to bed.

"Has Sara heard from Pietre lately?"

"I don't think so, not recently in any event. Why?"

"It is just that it is so incredibly bad on the Eastern Front for all the men. Most of the officers have only youths to command, and it must be mentally and physically debilitating for them without hardly any food or ammunition. At least the dreadful weather is over, and they are not freezing. I am sure that they will still be in a stalemate situation next winter, however. I hope Pietre can be transferred to another field hospital."

"You sound really worried, Sigmund, have you heard something?"

"Only that one or two senior officers have had complete breakdowns."

"I will check with Sara tomorrow." We settled down, but I had a very disturbed night thinking of Pietre.

The following morning I got going early and went to see Sara.

"Hi! You're an early bird," she said Sara when she opened the door.

"It is just that we wondered if you had heard from Pietre?"

"No, I haven't heard for quite a while. Have you heard something?" Sara looked concerned.

"Nothing definite, but Sigmund has heard that some senior officers have had complete breakdowns due to the extreme lack of food, ammunition, and unexperienced soldiers. Most of those that have been sent to replace casualties are little more than young boys. Can Pietre not get transferred to a field hospital away from the Eastern Front? Sigmund and Frederick are going to see if there is anything that can be done. There is a big military hospital not far from Berlin that is very short of experienced medical staff."

"That would be wonderful but, of course, I would be better pleased if he could come home for a while, but anything other than the Eastern Front would be a blessing."

"Let's hope that Sigmund and Kristofer can do something helpful," I said.

"Anyway, come round to dinner tonight and stay over so we can have a drink. I will check the church on my way home to see if there is a message for us."

I hugged Sara and set off for the church. When I got there, the thin, haggard man was there that we had seen before and given food to.

"I am so glad to see you. We need a message sent as soon as possible. It is thought that an attempt will be made to assassinate Churchill by someone who has infiltrated the inner echelons of the war office. We don't know who it is, but it will be someone fairly new to the post they are in. It is definitely a male of around thirty or forty years of age, educated in England but German by birth."

"I will do this immediately," I said and ran back to my house. Sara was startled when I burst into the house.

"Get the radio. I must send an urgent radio message. I will take the radio away from here so you will not be implicated."

"I want to come with you, Nicole."

"No, definitely not. It is too risky. I have to be in the best situation possible to make sure the message gets through, and there are many SS patrols around at the moment."

We both set about getting the radio out of the oven, and I lost no time in getting down the slope and running up the tract to the spot where we knew messages would get through because of its proximity to the Nazi radio station, very dangerous but necessary. I sent the message twice in code, and as I started packing up the radio, I felt the barrel of a gun at the back of my head.

"Stand up," shouted the soldier while pushing the nozzle of the gun painfully into my head. I stood up, and he pushed me away from my radio while another soldier picked it up. Several soldiers, one of whom was an officer, surrounded me. There was quite a discussion going on and eventually the officer addressed me.

"Frau Lubisch, what are you doing here? Why are you sending messages by radio?"

I did not answer but just glared as bravely as possible at him. He pushed me roughly into the midst of the rest of the patrol, and I was frogged-marched up the track and manhandled unceremoniously into the back of a truck. My clothes had ridden up, leaving nothing to the imagination and causing great hilarity amongst the troops.

Chapter 36

I was driven to La Rochelle and put into a cell in the basement of a large mansion, which looked as if it were built for people such as myself to be incarcerated, questioned, and probably tortured. I prayed that Sigmund would not admit to knowing that I was a resistance member. I was not visited by anyone for what seemed hours, but eventually the door opened and Sigmund came in accompanied by two SS officers. He was handcuffed and had obviously been beaten or worse.

"This is your wife, isn't it?" said the shortest of the two officers. The shorter the man, it seemed, the more vicious. Sigmund did not answer but just smiled at me and mouthed, "I love you."

"I love you, too," I said out loud. Sigmund was dragged out of the cell, and the door was slammed shut. Shortly after, a member of the Gestapo visited me.

"Who were you radioing?" I said nothing and received a blow from the butt of his gun to my left cheek, which was so powerful I felt my bone crack. I tried not to make a sound but my eyes watered and the Gestapo officer smirked. "Whom were you sending the radio message to?"

I did not answer and this incurred an almighty blow across the front of my legs, which buckled, and I fell to the floor, where I was kicked several times in the stomach. This made me vomit and urinate, and my face was rubbed in the stinking mess. The Gestapo officer left the cell and left me lying on the floor. I must have slept because when he next entered the cell, the sound made me jump.

"Ha! You are looking forward to my visit I see." I did not answer. "Can you not speak, Frau Lubisch, or are you too stupid to realise that I will make you speak? It would be so much more pleasant if we had a reasonable conversation."

I did not answer. He opened the door and beckoned someone to come in. A burly, cruel-looking man entered, and a chair was put in the middle of the room.

"Take off you dress." I ignored the request. "I said, take off your dress."

Again I ignored the request. The burly brute tore off my dress as though it were tissue paper. A bucket of freezing water was thrown over me and my legs were tied to the back legs of the chair, dragging my legs wide apart and exposing my undergarments. I must be insane because I thought to myself, *Thank goodness I have nice lacy knickers on*, and I giggled. This was rewarded by a smash in the face, probably breaking my nose.

"If you do not answer our questions, you and your husband will be punished severely," the first Gestapo officer said.

I felt such a pang of remorse that I was the cause of whatever Sigmund was going through. For his sake, I must not weaken. The questions were asked over and over, and I never answered one. I was beaten, burnt with cigarettes, dowsed with water, kicked and sexually abused, and all the time I tried to keep a look of contempt on my face, mainly by thinking of the people who had been sent to Auschwitz and Bergen-Belson. Every part of me was in severe pain. As I lay on the floor sideways, still tied to the chair, a couple of brutes entered and thrust some implement or other into my vagina and administered electric shocks. Mercifully, I passed out.

The next thing I saw was Sigmund sitting on the floor opposite me with tears streaming down his black-and-blue, battered face as I received more electric shocks, again causing me to thankfully fall into oblivion. How many days and nights Sigmund and I were tortured, I did not know or care, but I did not answer one question. I knew I had been there for some time as I was thin, stinking, and in agony. At last the Gestapo had the sense to realise that I was not going to answer any of their questions, and I was dragged out into a courtyard where Sigmund was being held up by ropes attached to rings in the wall unable to stand unaided.

"You think you are so smart, don't you? Nothing will stop us winning the war and you have suffered unnecessarily, but nothing will make you suffer more than this." Two soldiers dragged me over to Sigmund.

"Shoot him. Shoot him. This is an order," they shouted in my face as they forced a gun into my hand.

"Please do as they say, my darling," Sigmund said. "I love you."

"I love you too, Sigmund, with all my heart." As I said this, I raised the gun very slowly. I was nearly too weak to hold it, but I managed to get it above my waist and quickly placed it under the roof of my mouth. I pulled the trigger.

Chapter 37

When the war was over Sara and Pietre went to see Nicole's parents. They already knew that their daughter was very brave and had saved many lives, but they knew little of her husband, Sigmund. Sara brought along photographs of both of them showing how deliriously happy they had been. They told them about the children Sara and Sigmund had managed to get out of Auschwitz and showed them letters of those who had been saved and who had written expressing their undying gratitude and their great sadness when they learnt the fate of Sigmund and Nicole. Obviously Sigmund had been executed.

In the little town of Blois, Nicole's parents, Sara and Pietre, a contingent representing the Jewish community, and many of the locals erected a memorial to mark the unbelievable bravery of Nicole and Sigmund.

Prologue

David Isaac eventually was adopted by a couple in the United States and became a senator in the state of Wisconsin.

Sylvia, the little "skivvy," was taken to Eire and adopted by a farming family. Sylvia married one of the sons and had six children.

The two sisters, Ada and Felisberta, after getting to England were found by distant relations and went to live in Golders Green. Ada became a teacher and Felisberta a doctor.

Major Sinclair had a prosthetic lower leg and worked at Bletchley Park as a code breaker and then went on to the Ministry of Defence.

Ruth went to a family in Kent, but unfortunately died with the rest of the family during an air raid.

On his arrival in England, Jacob, too, was adopted by a wealthy, Jewish family. He attained educational excellence and went to Cambridge University, attaining a First in Law and is now a Queen's Council.

Review Requested:
If you loved this book, would you please provide a review at Amazon.com?
Thank You

Lightning Source UK Ltd.
Milton Keynes UK
UKOW02n2050210816

281132UK00004B/23/P